ON DANGEROUS
GROUND

Visit us at www.boldstrokesbooks.com

What Reviewers Say About
Bold Strokes Books

"With its expected unexpected twists, vivid characters and healthy dose of humor, *Blind Curves* is a very fun read that will keep you guessing."—*Bay Windows*

"In a succinct film style narrative, with scenes that move, a character-driven plot, and crisp dialogue worthy of a screenplay...the Richfield and Rivers novels are...an engaging Hollywood mystery...series."—*Midwest Book Review*

Force of Nature "...is filled with nonstop, fast paced action. Tornadoes, raging fire blazes, heroic and daring rescues... Baldwin does a fine job of describing the fast-paced scenes and inspiring the reader to keep on turning the pages." —*L-word.com Literature*

In the Jude Devine mystery series the "...characters seem fully capable of walking away from the particulars of whodunit and engaging the reader in other aspects of their lives."—*Lambda Book Report*

Mine "...weaves a tale of yearning, love, lust, and conflict resolution...a believable plot, with strong characters in a charming setting."—*JustAboutWrite*

"While these two women struggle with their issues, there is some very, very hot sex. If you enjoy complex characters and passionate sex scenes, you'll love *Wild Abandon*."— *MegaScene*

"*Course of Action* is a romance...populated with a host of captivating and amiable characters. The glimpses into the lifestyles of the rich and beautiful people are rather like guilty pleasures...a most satisfying and entertaining reading experience."—*Midwest Book Review*

The Clinic is "...a spellbinding novel."—*JustAboutWrite*

"*Unexpected Sparks* lived up to its promise and was thoroughly enjoyable...Dartt did a lovely job at building the relationship between Kate and Nikki."—*Lambda Book Report*

"*Sequestered Hearts*...is everything a romance should be. It is teeming with longing, heartbreak, and of course, love. As pure romances go, it is one of the best in print today." —*L-word.com Literature*

"*The Exile and the Sorcerer* is a mesmerizing read, a tour-de-force packed with adventure, ordeals, complex twists and turns, and the internal introspection of appealing characters."— *Midwest Book Review*

The Spanish Pearl is "...both science fiction and romance in this adventurous tale...A most entertaining read, with a sequel already in the works. Hot, hot, hot!"—*Minnesota Literature*

"A deliciously sexy thriller...*Dark Valentine* is funny, scary, and very realistic. The story is tightly written and keeps the reader gripped to the exciting end."—*JustAbout Write*

"*Punk Like Me*...is different. It is engaging. It is life-affirming. Frankly, it is genius. This is a rare book in that it has a soul; one that is laid bare for all to see."—*JustAboutWrite*

"*Chance* is not a novel about the music industry; it is about a woman discovering herself as she muddles through all the trappings of fame."—*Midwest Book Review*

Sweet Creek "...is sublimely in tune with the times." —*Q-Syndicate*

"*Forever Found*...neatly combines hot sex scenes, humor, engaging characters, and an exciting story."—*MegaScene*

Shield of Justice is a "...well-plotted...lovely romance...I couldn't turn the pages fast enough!"—Ann Bannon, author of *The Beebo Brinker Chronicles*

The 100th Generation is "...filled with ancient myths, Egyptian gods and goddesses, legends, and, most wonderfully, it contains the lesbian equivalent of Indiana Jones living and working in modern Egypt."—*Just About Write*

Sword of the Guardian is "...a terrific adventure, coming of age story, a romance, and tale of courtly intrigue, attempted assassination, and gender confusion...a rollicking fun book and a must-read for those who enjoy courtly light fantasy in a medieval-seeming time."—*Midwest Book Review*

"*Of Drag Kings and the Wheel of Fate*'s lush rush of a romance incorporates reincarnation, a grounded transman and his peppy daughter, and the dark moods of a troubled witch—wonderful homage to Leslie Feinberg's classic gender-bending novel, *Stone Butch Blues*."—*Q-Syndicate*

Wall of Silence "...is perfectly plotted and has a very real voice and consistently accurate tone, which is not always the case with lesbian mysteries."—*Midwest Book Review*

In *Running with the Wind* "...the discussions of the nature of sex, love, power, and sexuality are insightful and represent a welcome voice from the view of late-20-something characters today."—*Midwest Book Review*

"Rich in character portrayal, *The Devil Inside* is an unusual, unpredictable, and thought-provoking love story that will have the reader questioning the definition of right and wrong long after she finishes the book."—*JustAboutWrite*

ON DANGEROUS GROUND

by

D.L. Line

2009

ON DANGEROUS GROUND
© 2009 By D.L. Line. All Rights Reserved.

ISBN 10: 1-60282-113-5
ISBN 13: 978-1-60282-113-2

This Trade Paperback Original Is Published By
Bold Strokes Books, Inc.
P.O. Box 249
Valley Falls, NY 12185

First Edition: August 2009

CREDITS
Editors: Cindy Cresap and Stacia Seaman
Production Design: Stacia Seaman
Cover Design By Sheri (graphicartist2020@hotmail.com)

Acknowledgments

This story, my first real attempt at a novel, would never have happened without the combined input of quite a few people. I am indebted to all of you. Come by sometime. I'll make you dinner.

First and foremost, huge thanks to Chris Cheshire, my best friend and confidant. You're so much more than that, but we can talk about it when you get home from work.

To Emma, Dudie, and Adam, for being cool peeps. Thanks for trying to understand this madness that I do.

To Paul Line, Detective/Arson Investigator (retired), Hamilton (Ohio) Police Department, my technical advisor, as well as the best dad a gal could ever want. Thank you for teaching me how to shoot a gun, how to set a house on fire, and how to talk to people. That means a lot to me.

To Rita Line, my mom, the person who told me that I could be anything I want. I'm not sure that this was exactly what you had in mind, but thanks for believing in me anyway.

To my brother, Tom, for taking me to the range and the gun show and for making sure that I armed the FBI appropriately. Thanks for all the movies and everything else you've ever done.

To my friends on the KB, for reading and encouraging my work. Thanks for all of your comments and support.

Finally, to all of the folks at Bold Strokes, especially Cindy Cresap, my editor. You kicked me in the ass, and I didn't always like it, but the results speak for themselves. Thank you.

Dedication

To Chris, who makes all of this possible. Thank you.

CHAPTER ONE

FBI Agent Terri McKinnon ran as if her life depended on it, feet pounding through puddles just deep enough to slow her progress. Terri's partner, Agent Robert C. Kraft, known to the world as Bobby, splashed through the puddles behind her. A suspect, a kid of really not much more than fifteen or sixteen, ran as if his life depended on it, until he was stopped at the end of the alley, progress impeded by ten vertical feet of chain link fence and a rather greasy-looking Dumpster.

Terri kept running, closing the distance, while the perpetrator in the ratty field coat appeared to weigh his options. Reaching to the small of her back, she tucked her SIG Sauer P-228 automatic handgun into its holster, freeing up her hands. The perp climbed up and slid on the slick surface of the Dumpster, fighting against his own feet, attempting to reach the fence, but he never made it as Terri caught the hem of his coat and yanked hard. She watched him tumble backward and braced for the collision as his body came crashing down, driving her from her feet, knocking her flat on her back with a splash in a nearby puddle. Dripping wet, Terri grabbed the kid by the jacket and started pounding the shit out of him.

"You shot her, you bastard." She raised her fist to strike the kid again. She wanted to kill him, but something stopped her.

"Terri." She heard the male voice, demanding her attention. "Agent McKinnon, pay attention."

"What?"

Bobby loomed over her with his hands on his hips. "Get your head back in the game, Terri."

Lying on a dry mat, looking up at the bright mercury vapor lights of a gymnasium, Terri blinked, clearing her head of the vivid memory. "Sorry, Bobby. You're right. I lost my focus. Let's try that again." Accepting the hand that was offered, she pulled herself up off the mat, squared her shoulders, lowered her stance, and pulled her thoughts out of the rainy alley and back into the workout. Bobby faked right, but Terri saw it coming. She stepped in quickly, threw a leg behind his knee, and pushed, tripping him and sending all six feet, five inches of him crashing backward hard into the mat.

"Time," he gasped, crossing the palm of his right hand with the extended fingers of his left. "Good shot, sweetie." She continued to wait, bouncing lightly on the balls of her feet, as Bobby struggled for the wind that she'd quite effectively knocked out of him. "Terri, relax. I need a second here."

She stopped smiling and bouncing. Terri hated it when Bobby couldn't keep up. Truth be told, she pretty much hated anything that gave her too much time to think, but the physical training was necessary to ensure that she stayed ready for anything. She went to a nearby bench and grabbed two towels and two bottles of water. She tossed one of each to Bobby, and opened the water. "Bobby, you're getting too old for this."

He laughed and sat up. "Bullshit. I'm only thirty-one, same as you. That was just a lucky shot."

Terri glared at him. "Lucky shot, my ass." She continued

to glare and waited for the sarcastic return shot that she knew from experience was coming.

"What? You're kidding, right?" She shook her head as he continued. "You're saying that if I stay home every night, read, and talk to my cat, that I'll be what? Faster? Stronger? Boring?"

"Hey, I'm not boring. I prefer to think of myself as introspective." She put her hands on her hips and continued to defend her choices. "So stop trying to convince me that just because my social schedule is, well, light—"

"More like nonexistent."

Undaunted, she ignored his little comment and wiped the sweat from the back of her neck. "My social calendar is my business. We've had this conversation plenty of times over the last seven years. I come and go as I please, and I like the quiet. You act like because I've been single for a while—"

He interrupted again, holding up a hand, wiggling his fingers for emphasis. "Five years."

"Wow," she answered, a little surprised. Had it really been that long? "Five years, huh? Good thing one of us is keeping score." She wanted to laugh, but that wasn't how she felt. Five years. It was a long time to miss someone. Bobby must have seen the shift in her demeanor.

"Sorry, sweetie. I didn't mean to bring it up."

"What?"

Bobby gave her his best I-don't-believe-you face. "Terri, I know the look, the one that you get when you think about what happened. It wasn't your fault."

Bobby was only concerned because he wanted her to be happy, and she knew it. He'd made this fact abundantly clear during their time working together, but she certainly didn't feel like discussing it during a workout. "C'mon, Agent Kraft. On your feet. Let's settle this thing."

He finally caught his breath. "Are you sure?"

She waved him off. "I need to work it out. I'm fine."

"Okay then." Bobby assumed a fighting stance and waggled his eyebrows. "So, Agent McKinnon, do you want to make it interesting?"

"Sure. What did you have in mind?"

"If I knock you on your ass, you go out with me tomorrow night. I might have a date for you."

Oh, this was beginning to get scary. "Might? What the hell does that mean, might? Oh, God, I hate to think what kind of poor defenseless girl you've cajoled into going out with you…I mean me." She crouched back down, ready to go, and stopped, standing back upright. "Hey, wait. What do I get if I knock you on your ass?"

He thought for a second and brightened as an idea formed. "How about this? If you win, I pick you up and drive you home for a week. Then you don't have to ride the Metro."

No DC Metrorail commuter headaches for a week. Terri liked the idea. "Okay, I'm sold. Let's go." She crouched, ready to pounce, and Bobby mirrored her stance. "On three…"

She got as far as two, and Bobby jumped. With no time to react, she hit the floor hard, mad as hell. "Hey! You cheated."

"Too bad." He got up and loomed over her, smiling, while she stayed on the floor and fumed. "I'll pick you up, tomorrow night at seven. Dress nice, okay?" He didn't wait for her to answer. He just turned away, picked up his stuff, and headed for the locker room, waving and calling back as he left. "Have a nice ride home on the train."

❖

The Metro escalator emptied out into the lights and bustle of the Dupont Circle area of Washington, DC. Terri walked north on Connecticut Avenue, past Lambda Rising books, and over to Twentieth Street toward the townhouse that she shared with her cat, Jojo. "Just an accident," she muttered when she caught her reflection in the bookstore window. She wanted to believe it. "Sick twist of fate." Why shouldn't she believe it? The FBI did. Bobby was there. He saw what happened and he believed it, too. "Wrong place at the wrong time. Nothing more." Terri shook her head and kept walking. She opened her front door and found herself greeted with a cheery "meow" and fuzzy figure eights around her legs. "Jojo!" She greeted her with a scratch to the ears as she dropped her computer bag on the chair just inside the door. "C'mon, kiddo, you must be hungry."

Jojo commenced the figure eight motion once again, almost tripping her in the process of scooping kibble. Terri left the cat to happily crunch away at her dinner while she leaned over to remove her sensible black work shoes and swore at the ever-present white cat hair around the hems of her black suit pants.

"Dammit, cat. Why can't you just not shed?" Terri mused inwardly that maybe if she could wear something else, like something with color of any kind, cat hair wouldn't be a problem.

Terri went up the steps to her bedroom to change, but flopped down on the side of her bed instead. She stared at her closet, mostly loaded with identical black jackets, black pants, and white shirts. She kept a few casual items of clothing for the occasional night out that Bobby forced her to endure, but these were often left hanging in the closet for long, uninterrupted spaces of time. Besides, casual clothing that was the least bit fashionable made it terribly difficult to conceal the automatic handgun that she was required to carry on her person at all times.

Alyssa had hated the fact that Terri always had to carry a gun. Said it gave her the willies. Terri removed her weapon from the belt holster at the small of her back, unloaded it, and placed the weapon and ammo in the top drawer of the dresser. Terri hauled herself off the edge of the bed and peeled off her work clothes. Her usual uniform at home, a loose pair of red sweatpants and an oversized "Brutus the Buckeye" T-shirt, seemed like the best idea. She dressed and headed back down to start water on the stove for tea. While she waited for the water to boil, she thought about the mess she'd managed to let herself get tricked into for tomorrow night. A night out with Bobby usually meant she'd wind up walking home alone after he hooked up with some cute boy thing, but a blind date was worse.

Instead of walking home alone, she'd managed to get herself trapped into a night out that she wasn't interested in, followed by walking someone else to the Metro, and then walking home alone. Shaking her head, she bent over to talk to the cat. "Jojo, I know he's my best friend, but will this never end?"

Jojo answered simply by using more figure eight motions to deposit white fur around the elastic bottoms of the red sweatpants.

CHAPTER TWO

The code stretched across the width of the twenty-one-inch monitor and extended several inches down its length. To the uninformed it looked like pure nonsense, but it was the art of Jennifer Rosenberg. A resident of the tiny village of Mount Crawford, Virginia, Jen loved the peace of living nestled in the Shenandoah Valley, with its rocky hillsides full of cows and spectacular views of both the Blue Ridge and Appalachian Mountains. She'd had enough of big city life to finally move her consulting practice to the restored farmhouse that she shared with Snickers, a pug-Chihuahua mix of indeterminate origin. Both friend and early warning system, Snickers had the ferocity of a rottweiler packed into a twelve-pound body. Not that he could do a lot of damage if someone seriously wanted past him, but they were in for a fight as far as he was concerned.

Jen checked the code one last time. Certain that it was safely running on its own, she left the converted downstairs bedroom/office that contained two desktop systems, two laptops, a router for the satellite uplink, a small server for additional space, and a twin bed. Jen usually just curled up with Snickers on the office bed while some important code ran so she could tend to it immediately when the beep that signaled its completion woke her up.

"C'mon, little dude, let's get you some dinner." Jen headed for the kitchen, but stopped when her phone vibrated in the pocket of her cargo pants.

She removed the offending device and checked the display for the identity of the caller.

Joe Edwards was Jen's oldest friend. A classmate from public school, Joe had been her one and only boyfriend for exactly three weeks in the tenth grade. The fact that Joe liked Jen and Jen liked girls added up to one completely disastrous romantic relationship, but a truly fast friendship. Joe was a carpenter by trade, and he frequently worked at the busy Hollywood studios building both location and soundstage sets.

Joe always sounded happy when he called. "Hey, farm girl! Just confirming my ride from that poor little excuse for an airport down the road from you. Are we still on for my little skiing adventure Friday?"

"Of course, doofus. You think I'd make you walk? And I am not a farm girl." She paused, contemplating her last statement. "Well, not really, but then again, I do own a farm—"

"Jen, stay with me." Joe laughed and continued, "Anyway, I've seen more than one horse and buggy in that godforsaken place that you call home. I just had to ask."

"Hey, you know those are Mennonite farmers, and most of the people around here drive real cars. Well, I guess they're real cars, if you call a '65 Chevy pickup truck with a gun rack in the rear window and a fifty/fifty ratio of Bondo to rust a car, but you know what I mean."

"Yeah, babble girl, I getcha. Just had to give you a little shit for bailing on me. But then again, at least you decided to settle somewhere close to a ski resort, so it's all good."

"Of course I did. I knew you'd never come see me if I didn't offer some special amenities. I can't offer you any hustle or even a little bit of bustle, so I had to settle for manmade snow and Civil War battlefields as far as the eye can see."

"I know, Jen, it's everything we've ever dreamed of." Jen could practically hear the rolling of his eyes, but she knew he was only giving her a hard time.

"Hey, nothing but the best for you," Jen said while she cradled the phone to her ear to look for the paper where she had scribbled the arrival information for his flight. "You'll be here at seven forty-three p.m. on US Air flight 3462, barring weather complications or cows on the runway."

"Yep, that's it. Barring bovine intervention." Jen groaned at the really bad pun, said her good-byes, and hung up.

Jen leaned over with her hands on her knees in order to talk to her little dog pal. "C'mon, Snicker-man, let's check that code one more time and get this place ready for company."

CHAPTER THREE

Terri opted for a V-neck sweater and a heavy, dark floral print skirt. The sapphire-colored sweater did wonderful things to accent the color of her eyes, and the roominess of the skirt provided adequate cover for the leg holster that held her service weapon. She would, of course, flash anyone within view if the concealed handgun was needed, but that couldn't be helped.

"It just makes me uncomfortable," Alyssa had said on more than one occasion. She always left the room when Terri had to load or unload it. Too bad Terri couldn't get to it quickly enough the one time that she really needed to.

"Terri, drop it," she said quietly to herself while she fixed her collar in the mirror. She stepped into her navy blue Dansko clogs, choosing comfort over style based on the amount of walking that she knew was inevitable at the end of her evening. As she checked her conservative application of makeup one last time, the doorbell rang. She bounded down the stairs, opened the door, and was greeted by the smiling face of Bobby on the porch with his hands in the pockets of his leather jacket.

He wasn't even fully in the door before speaking as he checked out Terri's clothing selection. "Oh, nice. Good choice." He made a spinning motion with his right index finger pointed toward the floor. "Twirl for me."

Terri did as instructed, making one revolution so he could appraise her outfit. "Well…?" she asked.

"It's good, kiddo. Might even get you laid." Bobby thought for a moment before continuing, "But I don't know that I've ever heard of come-fuck-me clogs. Not so sure about that part."

Terri rolled her eyes. "Well, me getting laid is not what this is about. You know, we've had this conversation a dozen times. My one and only objective is getting home from the Metro in relative comfort."

Bobby sighed. "Terri, why don't you just try to keep an open mind? Mindy just might be the girl of your dreams."

"Mindy? A bookstore chickie named Mindy from Rat's Ass, Wisconsin, is at very little risk of becoming the girl of my dreams. What are you thinking?"

"First, I'm thinking glass houses because you're from Rat's Ass, Ohio, if I'm not mistaken, and second, I'm thinking that you're the best friend a large fag from Virginia Beach could ever ask for. Go feed your kitty, grab your coat, and let's go. We're meeting them at the restaurant."

❖

Bobby and Terri walked the three blocks to the restaurant in their usual fashion: Bobby cruising the younger male denizens of the Circle, Terri nodding and agreeing with him. This time was always hard for her. It gave her time to think because all Bobby needed from her to keep the conversation lively was a strategically placed "mmm" or "yeah, he's hot" and he could amuse himself for hours. Not that he was self-centered, because he was one of the most unselfish and giving people that Terri had ever known. It was just that Bobby spent his days in his comfortable closet at work and only released his inner gay boy when they were out on the town. Well, once in a while at work, but never in front of anyone else. Added to this was the fact that she had been down this road before with him, and it never ended well. It hadn't ever ended all that badly, either; it just wasn't what she was looking for.

Around most people, Terri was quiet. Not in a hide-from-the-world kind of way, more in a deeply contemplative and extremely professional kind of way. When she was at work, she always thought about the job. When Jojo's food hit the bowl every evening, the job was still there. Evenings, weekends—none of that mattered, because Terri was, first and foremost, a cop. To protect and serve, and that was what she needed to do. The job was easier when the people you were protecting were strangers. She had also tried to do the dating thing Bobby's way, through a series of blind dates. Semi-disastrous blind dates. Since she wasn't going to risk loving someone and then losing her the way she had before, she opted to remain single, giving in and going out only when Bobby insisted. Terri was alone and coming to terms with the fact that alone was acceptable, even good. Besides, there was the Bureau to take care of her, keep her busy. She already knew that a personal life was hard enough to balance with the job, and her one lost relationship proved that girlfriends and FBI agents didn't mix. She left a tiny spark of hope alive, enough to keep her from freezing to death in her own thoughts, but not enough to spend time pining for things that would probably never happen.

Was she happy? Yes. Deliriously so? No, but who truly had that anyway? She had a beautiful home, a peaceful—if somewhat solitary—life, a good job, nice neighbors, and one really great pal. What else was necessary?

Terri had evidently misplaced an "mmm," forcing Bobby to stop in his tracks. He cocked his head and asked, "Have you heard anything I've said for the last block?"

She looked at him. "No. I'm sorry, just lost in my own head. Go on, please."

He shook his head and started over. "I was just telling you about Mindy and her buddy Daniel. He came here to go to school at Georgetown. She moved here to take her inner lesbian out for a walk in the big city, and now they work at the bookstore together. Got it?" She nodded for him to continue. "You and I are joining them for dinner, and maybe dancing—"

"Dancing?" Terri stopped dead in her tracks, shaking her head for emphasis. "I never agreed to dancing. Nope, no dancing."

"Aw, c'mon, Terri. I know you can shake your groove thing."

Pedestrians were starting to grumble as they had to shift to get around the pair on the sidewalk.

"I do not *have* a groove thing. No, Bobby, not this time. No dancing. I agreed to a simple dinner date to get you into some guy's pants. Nothing more."

Bobby pressed again, despite her warnings to the contrary, offering a compromise. "How about if we do the dinner thing, talk for a while, and then ask about the dancing? Does that work for you? It leaves you an opening to say no, and then Mindy can decide for herself if she wants to come to the bar with us or cut out when you do." He offered out his palms in a supplicating manner indicating that the ball was firmly in her court.

"Okay. Dinner, small talk, maybe coffee, and then I get to leave, right?"

"Yes, ma'am. That's it."

"Well, all right." She grabbed the sleeve of his jacket and pulled him along. "Let's get this over with."

❖

Thaiphoon was the newest and trendiest Asian fusion café on Dupont Circle. The yellow curry was everything the *Washington Post* critics claimed that it would be. Terri was even forced to admit that Mindy was far from the vacuous tramp that she'd been imagining all day. She was nice. Thankfully, she was smart as well. Enough to hold up her end of most conversations, but not quite enough to make Terri reconsider her no-dancing tirade from earlier. And Bobby had been gracious enough to pick up the entire dinner tab. As the conversation turned to plans of dancing, Terri mentally crossed her fingers in the hope that she could take her leave soon. It evidently worked. Mindy mentioned that some other bookstore employees were meeting at a bar and she had planned to join them. All in all, it appeared to be working out in everyone's favor.

As they were leaving the restaurant, Bobby motioned for the others to go ahead, that he'd catch up. Before Terri could turn to walk home, he gathered her in a fierce bear hug that lifted her feet from the ground. He asked if she would be all right walking home alone.

"Sweetie, I do it every night. Granted, it's not usually in a dress with a strap-on handgun, but I'll be fine. I promise."

He laughed heartily before turning to go. "See you Monday, then?"

"Yeah, Monday. Night, Bobby."

He was already running to catch up with the others and called over his shoulder, "You're the best, Terri."

She turned to walk home, muttering under her breath. "Yeah, I'm the best. That would certainly explain why it's Friday night in the gayest city on the eastern seaboard and I'm walking home alone."

Chapter Four

Jen stood on the long deck of the Massanutten Ski Resort, looking out across the trails of manmade snow. Rows of time-share condos lined the sides of the hills, providing a framework for the open ski trails, snowboarding stunt area, and a sculptured area for tube rides that looked like an amusement park slide. There was an assortment of brightly clad skiers, and she laughed at their antics, thinking that it was like having a front row seat for the live version of *America's Funniest Home Videos*. Who knew that the human body could be lifted off its skis, rendered completely airborne, and dropped forcefully onto the hard-packed snow in so many interesting and varied combinations? She winced as one more snowboarder, this one under a green, dragon-shaped hat, twisted in the air and landed on his shoulder with a sickening thud/grunt combination that Jen knew instinctively would keep him from phys ed class for at least a week. She allowed a small smile when she thought back to how she would have gratefully traded a minor injury for the terrors of PE class and communal high school showers.

"Wow, that's going to leave a mark," Joe said as he emerged from the lodge with two steaming cups of hot chocolate. He spoke to Jen, but his eyes remained locked on Mr. Dragon Hat as other skiers arrived to assess the damage. The kid waved off the attention and Joe turned to Jen and handed her one of the Styrofoam cups. "Here, this is for you."

Jen accepted the drink and peeled off the lid to blow across the top. "Thanks. How come you're not out there? Your knee bothering you again?"

"Yeah, a little." He stretched and flexed the offending joint. "I probably overdid it yesterday, and the two runs this morning were not so much fun. I need to take it easy."

"Well, if that means I get to spend the day with you, then I'm okay with it. As long as you're not in pain, 'cause then, well, selfish much?"

"Naahh, I really am okay. I know you're not being selfish. Maybe a little lonely?"

"Who, me?" she answered a little too quickly and turned away. False bravado was the most prevalent weapon in her arsenal, used to avoid the real issues of her solitary existence. "I'm fine here, all kinds of fine."

"C'mon, Jen, this is me. I've known you for long enough to know that you hate it out here. This middle-of-nowhere thing just isn't you. I know you love teaching at the college, but between that and the consulting thing, you never do anything. Not that there's anything to do around here. Hell, there's not even any women to go out with. You putter around your house in this self-imposed exile." Jen started to protest, but stopped when she realized that Joe was right. He went on. "And your best friend is a miniature psycho hell dog that apparently thinks I'm the antichrist."

"Well, he worries about me." Jen stubbornly refused to make eye contact.

"Well, I worry about you, too. I want you to be happy." He kept talking as he took her by the upper arm, prompting her to look at him. "I really want you to call me sometime soon and tell me that you've met a tall, striking brunette with blue eyes and glorious tits, and how she swept you off your feet and right into bed." He released her arm to punctuate his comments with hand gestures. "Then yadda, yadda, happily ever after, blah, blah, off into the sunset, etcetera. We both know that's what you want. You're just scared to admit it."

"And you, Joe Edwards, supportive buddy-o-mine, just want details." She noticed the blush creeping up his face as he averted his glance toward the ski slope. "Yeah, that's what I thought." She punched him on the arm.

He grabbed his arm in mock distress. "Hey, killer, easy with the butch there!"

"Oh, don't be such a baby!" She stared at the steamy cup in her hand. "The problem is that I know you're right. I do want that, or at least some variation of it. I've pretty much decided that it's not going to happen, though, and I guess that's okay, too. I'll work with what I have, for now. And I promise when Ms. Blue Eyes waltzes up to my front door and sweeps me off my feet, you'll be the first to know. Agreed?"

"Agreed." Joe protectively wrapped one arm around her shoulders, turned to place a small kiss on the top of her head, and spoke softly, adding one more thought. "Don't forget about the glorious tits part when you call."

"Joe! Ughh!" She wiggled to get out from under his arm. "You never stop, do you?"

"Nope, never."

CHAPTER FIVE

The Investigations Department, located on the second floor of the J. Edgar Hoover Building, looked like any number of nondescript offices in ordinary, featureless buildings that could be found just about anywhere along Pennsylvania Avenue. Terri sat and stared out the window while Bobby attempted to cajole her into a game of paper football across their desks. It wasn't going to happen. Their last case was all wrapped up, mission accomplished, and the boss was on his way up from a meeting. For Terri, that meant a new case. Something fresh to dive into. Sure beat the shit out of this downtime. It usually only lasted a matter of hours, but for Terri, it meant that dreaded time to think.

"Bobby—" She turned to ask him a question, but stopped when his latest attempt at a field goal caught her right square on the nose. She retrieved the paper football from the edge of her desk and shook it at him. "Hey! Watch it or I'm going set this thing on fire and stick it in your ear."

"Ooh, aren't we butch?" Bobby shot back while Terri tossed the paper in the trash. She wanted to give him shit for acting like a queen in the office, but no one was around, so she let it slide. Besides, she was getting impatient. Before it could get much worse, she heard the elevator ding in the hallway.

Supervisor George McNally, a thirty-year veteran of the

Bureau with a steel gray brush cut and the demeanor of a pit bull with a migraine, stepped purposefully from the hallway into the office. While crossing through the department toward his door, he used only five words to announce his intentions.

"McKinnon. Kraft. My office. Now."

McNally was never one to mince words. Terri and Bobby had heard that tone from their boss before. And when he said "now," he meant "right now." They exchanged a concerned glance and wondered what the hell might be up. Knowing that the answers would be revealed soon enough, they followed McNally into his office.

"Close the door, please, and have a seat."

Bobby ushered Terri fully into the office before reaching behind to close the door. They sat in matching gray central supply chairs and remained silent as McNally pressed forward.

"We may have a serial crime. I've got three seemingly unrelated murders in completely different parts of the country. Not unusual, except for the fact that the perp has some kind of number fetish and all of the victims work as consultants for one of those giant tech companies up the road in Herndon." He shoved a manila folder across his desk toward Bobby and Terri. "That's faxed copies of the crime scene reports."

Terri took the folder while McNally slid a second one across his desk to Bobby. "This one," he gestured toward the paperwork, "is the pertinent information you'll need about NoVaGenEx. That's the company that these folks used to work for. There's contact information for the company and a list of all of the other people who do the same consulting work. I know there's not a lot here to go on, but we're not here to speculate. We're here to investigate. So go do that. I'll expect a preliminary report by close of business Friday. That's tomorrow, by the way. Thank you."

Bobby and Terri both knew that when McNally said "thank you" he really meant "get out." They rose from their seats, Bobby opened the door, ushered Terri out, and closed the door behind him. Terri shook her head as she walked back to her desk. "He's always so charming."

Bobby laughed a little and answered, "Yeah, a real Miss Congeniality." He sat at his desk and opened his folder. "Wow, someone isn't fooling around." He pulled out a crime scene photo and tossed it across the desk.

Terri picked up the picture. "No kidding." The first thing she noticed was blood. Lots of it. "What happened here?"

Bobby leafed through the forensics reports. "Here it is. Single gunshot wound from point-blank range to the back of the neck."

She thought about it for a moment. "That means he snuck up from behind. This guy never would have known what hit him." Terri looked closer at the picture. "Here's that number thing McNally mentioned."

Bobby leaned across the desk while Terri showed him the photo. "Right here. Thirty-six, written in blood on the forehead. Is there something on the other two?"

He leafed through the photos on his desk and pulled out one of victim number two. "Yep, here it is." He tossed the picture to Terri.

"Eighty-nine? What on earth does that mean?"

Bobby looked as confused as Terri felt. "And what the fuck does it have to do with thirty-six?" He shuffled through the remaining pictures for victim number three. He found it. "Or forty-three?"

Terri picked up her pen to make a note. "I'll call the guys in crypto and see if they can come up with something."

"Sounds like a plan. Ooh, here's something else: the crime scenes were clean. No fibers, no usable footprints on the carpet, no prints, and that usually means latex gloves and hospital shoe covers. That requires some planning, unless, of course, the perp works in a hospital or research facility."

"Right. So that gives us anyone who has ever been to a hospital or had access to a drug store." She shook her head. "That really narrows it down. So, what about the weapon?"

Bobby scanned the report. "No casings, no slugs, just powder burns on the back of the neck. Coroner is speculating nine millimeter auto, but he won't swear to it. Too much bone and crap in the wound. And we've got to assume that he used a silencer. Vic number two lived in an apartment building, and no one heard a thing."

"Well, shit." Terri was frustrated. She stared at both pictures, trying to make sense out of it. It wasn't working.

"So, initial thoughts, Agent McKinnon?"

Terri leaned back in her chair. "Well, my first thought, considering that the victims work for the same company, would have been disgruntled employee, but this number thing kind of throws a monkey wrench into that theory."

"Always a classic, yes, but I agree. Not this time." Bobby rocked back in his chair with his hands behind his head. "Hey, maybe this company is into something." He motioned with his chin toward the folder in Terri's hands. "Tell me more about what they do."

"Let's see…" Terri nodded as she read. "Government contracts for software development, biotechnology, robotics, all kinds of stuff."

"That adds terrorism and blackmail to the list of motives, which flies a little better with the level of premeditation we see here, so maybe the numbers are a code of some kind. Something to do with some project they're working on." Bobby sat back in his chair again and shook his head. "Also, is this a solo act, or are we thinking multiple shooters?"

"Right…Georgia, Michigan, and Illinois aren't exactly next door to each other. We need to look at this closer."

"Okey-dokey," Bobby said. "How about I take the police reports and you call the tech-heads? Then we'll see what we can piece together," he paused to look at his watch, "in the next twenty-nine hours."

Terri nodded and opened her folder to get the phone number for the department manager of offsite operations at NoVaGenEx. Once she went through all the niceties and explained her need for information, she asked for a rundown of the consultant network.

"You see, Agent McKinnon, the use of independent consultants reduces the expense of providing workspace and health insurance benefits for a number of employees. It also serves as a way for us to decentralize a portion of our government contract work as a deterrent to cyber terrorism. I'm sure you can understand, especially in this day of government terror alerts, why this is of great importance to us. That's why the consultants are really not employees of NoVaGenEx, but they are well paid and fully compensated for any special hardware or software that might be required. Additionally, as independent contractors, no person knows anything about any other contractor, and we try to maintain a strategic geographical distribution of our consultant network as another firewall against cyber crime."

Terri nodded and scribbled a few notes. "Makes sense. So, we need to know if the three consultants that were targeted were working on the same project."

"No, I'm afraid that they weren't. NoVaGenEx maintains a network of over eight hundred consultants, and we usually run twenty, up to thirty different projects at a time."

Terri scratched "disgruntled employee" from her list. Just a hunch. "Okay then, thank you for your time. I have your contact information, so we'll be in touch if we need any further information. Please feel free to give me a call if you think of anything else you might believe to be pertinent." She concluded the call and looked toward Bobby, who was still on the phone.

Terri still had little information with which to start building a profile, so she moved on to the next step. It was essential to determine who had access to the employee list. A consultant leak at the company or outside hackers at work would make things immensely more complicated, so she broke down the list of consultants to try to uncover any connection between those people and the cities where the crimes had been committed. She started scanning the list but stopped when Bobby hung up the phone.

"That was Atlanta. They were crime scene number two. They've got nothing new, but I have a contact name and e-mail." He held up his legal pad to show Terri. "Victim number one is from Ann Arbor, Michigan. I talked to them and they've got nothing, either. I still need to call Joliet, Illinois, but I bet it's the same." He smiled and peeked over at Terri's notes. "Did you get anything?"

She tossed her pad to him. "I know that NoVaGenEx is a huge company, and how the consultant network is organized, but it really doesn't give us anything new to work with. Certainly nothing to establish a pattern."

"Well, shit." Bobby ruffled his hair in frustration while he looked at Terri's notes. "Are you looking for connections on that list there?"

"Yeah, and I only have two really loose ones to start with. I'll keep digging, but at least it's a place to start."

"Agreed." Bobby kept looking at Terri's notes, but stopped. "What's this mean?" He pointed to the notepad. "Homeland?"

"Oh, that." Terri reclaimed her notes. "That guy from the company made some noise about cyber terrorism, so I thought I'd have the computer geeks check our killer's artwork against the Homeland Security database. Maybe it's some kind of terror organization trying to shake things up."

"Hell, it could be the Knights of Columbus for all we know." Bobby looked frustrated.

Terri nodded. Sarcastic or not, he was right. "No shit, Bobby." She sighed. "Once you're finished with the locals in Illinois, will you call Denver?" She wrote down a name and tore off the paper. "Get someone out to talk to this consultant person." She tossed the paper on Bobby's desk. "She's on the NoVaGenEx list, she went to grad school at Emory University in Atlanta, and she lives just outside of Denver in Aurora now. Maybe she knows the vics from college or something like that."

Bobby picked up the paper. "Sure thing, Terri. Who are you calling?"

Phone in hand, Terri looked at her notes. "I've got a graduate of the University of Michigan who is now located in Mount Crawford, Virginia."

Bobby piped in, "Hey, I know where that is. I used to live right down the road from there."

"That's right. You went to school at James Madison, right? That's what this gal does, well, besides the consulting thing. She's an associate professor in the information systems department." She thought for a moment. "Bobby, this is only two hours from here, right?" Bobby nodded. "I'd feel better if we took care of this one ourselves."

Bobby leaned forward and rested his forearms on the desk. "When?"

"Sooner the better, don't you think?" She worked the timetable in her head. "How about tomorrow morning?"

Bobby grinned. "That would work. We can talk to your consultant, check in with the guys in Denver, and e-mail our plan to McNally by tomorrow afternoon."

"Great," Terri replied, "I'll go drop the idea on McNally's head, see if he'll go for it. I'm pretty sure he'd prefer to keep it in house rather than calling Richmond. He's closer to it that way too."

"Yeah, and speaking of McNally, he's going to need some press release stuff from this. I think we should keep the number thing out of it."

"Yes, definitely." Terri nodded adamantly. "It has to mean something. One copycat with a random number, and the whole thing is blown."

"Agreed, Agent McKinnon. Call your consultant and see if tomorrow morning works."

Terri looked back to her list for the name that she needed. She always felt better about a case when she could jump right in and do all of the initial leg work herself.

Jennifer Rosenberg. Nice name. Terri made the call.

CHAPTER SIX

Jen pulled her green SUV into the gravel drive of her house. She was still a little miffed from yet another confrontation with a student who seemed to believe that six hours every day playing World of Warcraft made him a computer expert. Well, she assured herself, he would never make that mistake in her classroom again. She chuckled inwardly recalling the look on the geek's face—as well as the resultant laughter from the entire class—when she casually showed him that advanced Linux code had very little in the way of mystical qualities, but that he'd be her first call if she needed an enchanted sword for anything. She laughed again. "Rosenberg, you're kind of a bitch." That certainly wouldn't stop her from doing it again.

She entered the mudroom through the door on the side of the house. Snickers was waiting patiently for her until the door opened and he could launch himself at her legs. "Hey, little dude, glad to see me?"

Jen dropped the mail on the kitchen counter and scooped Snickers's leash and his favorite neon pink tennis ball out of the bowl by the door. "Let's head for the pond, Snick. It's been a long day."

She grabbed a bottle of water from the fridge and headed

out the back door. She gave the ball a mighty heave into the tall weeds of the field to get Snickers started in the right direction. The air was brisk but the sun warmed her as she followed the trail Snickers had left through the weeds. Jen found herself thinking about Joe. His last words to her before he boarded the plane home had been a reminder to call him when Ms. Right walked into her life. She looked around her property—ten acres of fallow fields and a small stand of trees, surrounded by her neighbors' working farms—and tried to imagine what kind of act of God was going to drop a gorgeous single lesbian on her front porch. Jen shook her head, laughed at Joe's eternal optimism, and headed toward the pond and Snickers.

The pond was of the spring-fed variety, bounded on three sides by dense overgrowth. A large birch tree grew on the open side of the small body of water. The spot was secluded and peaceful by day, but creepy at night. These days Jen had a difficult time believing in forces that could not be coded into software, but that was really nothing new. She had always been like that. Jen was all about the numbers. From her misspent youth at the University of Michigan to her current life of teaching and private work, Jen loved the numbers. Any numbers.

"That's probably why you're still single, you huge geek." Jen shook her head.

A rustling nearby startled her, but she smiled when she saw Snickers bounding happily through the underbrush, hoping to flush out a rabbit or two. Jen spotted the bright pink ball that he'd opted to ignore, picked it up, and put it in her pocket. Jen whistled to get Snickers's attention and tossed the ball the full length of the field that led away from the pond. He bolted after the ball until the rustling of squirrels in the underbrush drew him away from his toy. As much as she loved the little dog, she was becoming annoyed with him because she was starting to feel pretty stupid playing fetch by herself. She had a sudden flash of memory of her college girlfriend Beth saying much the same thing to her about their relationship. "Jenny, I can't do it all by myself. You're spending so much time with Brad and your computers it's like I don't exist. Are you sure you wouldn't rather just *be* with him?" Jen shuddered at the thought of Brad, computer genius and all-around creepy guy. She supposed Beth had been right. Their relationship did end soon after that particular argument, but it certainly wasn't because she wanted to be with Brad. Hell, she almost went to jail because of him.

"Dammit, Snickers, the point of playing fetch is for me to throw the ball and for you to go get it. It's just stupid if you aren't going to keep up your end." He stopped in the brush and turned to look at her. She picked up the ball and waggled it at him to make sure she had his attention and threw it again. He sped out of the tangled weeds and actually went to get the toy. He brought it back to her, and she was able to keep him interested in the game until they arrived at the back door. Snickers blasted into the house through the flexible dog door, Jen a few steps behind him. She was clumsily trying to remove one muddy shoe by the heel with the toe of the other one when her cell phone rang. She removed it from her pocket to check the caller ID.

US Govt. "What the hell?" For a second Jen debated letting it ring through to voicemail, but her curiosity was piqued. She flipped it open and answered. "Hello?" She began working on the removal of her second shoe, waiting for someone to respond.

"Jennifer Rosenberg, please." The voice was pleasant, decidedly female, and to the point.

"Yes, this is Jennifer Rosenberg. Can I help you?" She juggled the phone as she bent over to pick up her shoes and set them out on the step to dry.

"Dr. Rosenberg, this is Special Agent Terri McKinnon from the Federal Bureau of Investigation. Do you have a moment?"

"Um, sure. What's this about?" Jen was decidedly nervous, even though she was pretty confident she hadn't done anything to attract the attention of the feds.

The pleasant female voice continued, "Ma'am, your name came up in the course of an investigation through your work with NoVaGenEx. We'd like to come out to Mount Crawford and ask you a couple of questions."

"Okay," she answered, but she wasn't really sure that it was.

"Ma'am, I can assure you that you aren't in any trouble as far as the Bureau is concerned. May we come out to your house tomorrow, say about one o'clock?"

"Sure, that'd be fine. Do you need directions?"

"No, ma'am. We can get there on our own. See you at one o'clock, then. Thank you."

Before Jen could say anything else, the call was terminated from the other end. "Well, thank you too," she said with a hint of sarcasm to her voice. She closed the phone, returned it to her pocket, and called out, "Hey, Snickers! Have you been hacking into Pentagon stuff on the laptop again while I was gone?" He looked at her and cocked his head. "No, I guess you haven't. Well, let's call work and see if we can find anything out."

She went into the office to retrieve the phone number for her contact at NoVaGenEx. The phone call was much the same as the one from the FBI, full of assurances that she was not in trouble and that she should cooperate as much as possible.

This went a small way to calm her nerves, but not far enough. She had walked away from her last run-in with the FBI. She was pretty sure that she was in the clear this time, but once bitten, twice shy. The next twenty-three hours were going to be hell.

CHAPTER SEVEN

Jen awoke with a start and quickly realized she'd fallen asleep in the office again. Snickers was snuggled in at the back of her knees. He grumbled slightly as she rolled over to check the office clock. Nine fifteen. "Oh, good. We've got some time before the feds get here." She decided to put the final clean on the house after breakfast. That still left plenty of time for a shower before one o'clock. She didn't have a Friday class, which was really too bad because it might have given her something else to think about besides being nervous that the federal government was going to be knocking on her door in a matter of hours.

At exactly one o'clock, a large black SUV pulled off the dirt road and into the gravel drive. Jen watched out the office window as two agents, one male and one female, stepped out of their respective sides of the vehicle. She noticed that they were dressed almost exactly the same, in black suits, white shirts, black shoes, and dark sunglasses. The large man was wearing a tie, and the woman's shirt had the top two buttons undone. As they started walking from the car, Jen swore she could hear the opening strains of an old George Thorogood song in her head. These two certainly looked to be bad to the bone.

"Never guess they were cops, huh, buddy?" Jen asked

Snickers. She opted to wait in the office until they rang the doorbell. The bell sounded and Snickers went off, barking and skidding on the hardwood toward the door. She tried to shush him with her foot as she opened the door, but he stopped when he caught sight of the two agents. Jen thought that his behavior was weird because he usually tried to remove everyone's foot at the ankle, but the sight of the two cops on her front porch brought her back to reality.

"Jennifer Rosenberg?" the woman asked. Both agents held their identification wallets open so she could see that they were the genuine articles.

"That would be me." She opened the storm door and ushered them in. "I thought we could talk in the kitchen. There's more room to stretch out." She laughed a little because she was still nervous. She pointed through the living room toward the kitchen in the back. "It's just through there."

They strode past Jen as she held the front door for them. She followed them into the kitchen, tossing one errant glance toward Snickers. He was still silent, and the propeller action of his tail added to her confusion. The male agent's voice brought her back to the present. "Is something wrong, ma'am?"

She shook her head. "No, well, I'm not sure. Snickers"— she motioned to the dog—"hates everybody. Well, apparently everybody except you two. I just don't get it. He should be yapping and growling, but…"

The big guy laughed a little. "Maybe it's just good old-fashioned respect for the law."

Jen relaxed. "Yeah, maybe. It's just strange." She turned her attention back to the female agent, who had remained silent through the exchange. Jen was aware that she was being studied intently, making her even more nervous. The agent pressed on, indicating that it was time to get down to business.

"Thank you for seeing us so quickly, Dr. Rosenberg. I'm

Special Agent McKinnon and this," she motioned toward the big guy, "is Special Agent Kraft. We just have a few questions and hopefully won't have to take up too much of your time."

"Um, sure, whatever. Have a seat at the table. Can I get you both some coffee?"

"Thank you, ma'am, that'd be great," Agent Kraft answered. "Just black, please, for both of us." Jen busied herself in the kitchen as she collected three mugs from the cupboard, filled them, slid one in front of each agent, and took the third for herself, adding two spoons of sugar before sitting at the head of the table.

Jen was starting to feel like a bug under a glass. She was nervous, fiddling with the spoon in her coffee, but stopped when they reached up to remove their sunglasses. She was stunned for just a second when she caught the deep blue of Agent McKinnon's eyes. Jen was also perceptive enough to notice that she'd been busted taking a peek, so she returned to the deliberate stirring of her coffee.

Agent Kraft broke the silence. "Dr. Rosenberg, your name came up during the course of an investigation. There have been three murders involving NoVaGenEx consultants, one in Ann Arbor, Michigan, another three weeks later just outside Atlanta, and the third just outside of Chicago. We have reason to believe that they're related, so we're investigating anyone with prior ties to the locations."

A light went on over Jen's head, "Oh, and since I went to school in Ann Arbor and have the same relationship with NoVaGenEx, you thought I might have some insight that could help you?"

"Exactly," Agent McKinnon said. Jen braved another quick glance at her, mentally noting that if the FBI ever allowed her to let her hair down, she'd be absolutely stunning. Yep, that was the word, *stunning*.

Agent Kraft continued, "So if you know anything that would be of assistance, we'd certainly appreciate it." He removed a pad of paper and pen from his inside pocket.

Jen thought for a moment, stirred her coffee again, and looked up at Agent McKinnon. She freaked and overreacted. "My four years at Michigan were basically uneventful. Classes, computer lab, that kind of stuff. I didn't exactly have a busy social life. I don't think I pissed anyone off, not intentionally anyway, and certainly not enough for someone to decide to exact revenge on me and my coworkers, not like I even know who they are. I mean, NoVaGenEx intentionally keeps us separate. I don't even know how many people are working on the same project that I am. Some kind of geographical firewall, I suppose. I'm not even sure what the whole project is about. It's mostly pretty cryptic stuff. I don't know how much I can help you."

She stopped talking as she realized that Kraft and McKinnon were watching her with slack-jawed amazement, noting that she never once stopped even to take a breath during her statement. Agent Kraft seemed to recover first, and asked again, "Nothing, no spurned suitors, no run-ins with the law, anything?"

Something itched in the back of Jen's thoughts—*tell them about Brad*—but she brushed it aside, needing it to be irrelevant. "Nope, not a thing. I might have pissed off a couple of girls, you know, hitting on their girlfriends, but—" She stopped as both agents began writing furiously, Agent Kraft with his paper and pen and Agent McKinnon on her top-of-the-line PDA. Jen continued, "But I suppose that's all in your file, or whatever you have about my government clearances." She grinned weakly at Agent McKinnon, checking for any reaction, and looked back down into her coffee mug.

Agent Kraft looked up from his legal pad. "Well, I

suppose that's all we need for now. We just need to compile this information and e-mail it back to Washington. We'll be in Harrisonburg for at least a few more hours if you think of anything else."

Agent McKinnon handed her a business card that contained a cell phone number and e-mail address. She urged, "Anything at all, even if it seems irrelevant."

"I getcha…anything at all."

The agents stood, indicating that the interview was over. Agent McKinnon spoke first. "Dr. Rosenberg, thank you for your time. We'll be in touch if we need more." She extended her hand to Jen, who shook it, perhaps a little longer than necessary. She also accepted a much briefer handshake from Agent Kraft while Agent McKinnon gathered her things and put them in her briefcase. Jen ushered her guests to the door. She watched as they made the trip back across the front of the house before she finally closed the door and exhaled. She wasn't exactly sure whether she was relieved or a little sad that the visit was over.

She ducked back into her office, watching out the window to make sure that the cops were securly back in their black SUV. She grabbed her cell phone and hit the speed dial to call Joe. "Pick up, pick up…Shit!" The call rang into voicemail. "Joe, it's me…She was here. Gorgeous, blue eyes, brunette… Call me." She snapped the phone closed. "Not like it matters, huh, Snickers? Gal that looks like that's got to be seeing someone, right?" Snickers just looked at her like she was nuts and wagged his tail.

CHAPTER EIGHT

Terri stared out the window of the truck while Bobby drove back toward Harrisonburg. He was quiet, but Terri knew better. She could tell from the look on his face. The next move was hers. "Okay, Bobby, what's on your mind?"

"I was just thinking about Dr. Rosenberg."

Terri was confused. "Yeah, I remember. Small, kind of jumpy. I was there." The confusion remained. "I feel like she didn't give us very much, but I think there's something that she's not telling us. What about her?"

He stared back at Terri with an expression that led her to believe she was missing something important. "Kind of jumpy? She looked positively terrified."

"Jumpy, terrified, whatever." Terri waved it off and opened the cap on a bottle of water. "I'm sure some of it had to do with finding out about her coworkers that way, but there was something else. Not sure what—"

Bobby stared back and interrupted. "Not sure what besides how hard she was cruising you."

"Cruising me?" Terri sputtered and choked on her water. "What are you talking about?"

Bobby stared at Terri like she was insane. "Girl, you must be blind!"

"What are you talking about?"

"You can't really mean you didn't notice her checking you out."

Terri continued to stare at him, idly wondering if he might just sprout another head. She really hadn't noticed anything except for how nervous Dr. Rosenberg was acting. "No, Bobby, I didn't. I think you're delusional."

Bobby looked annoyed and waved her off. "Okay, time to profile. Here's how I see it." Terri sat back in her seat and prepared for the ritual listening.

Bobby took on his best professorial manner, ticking off items on his fingers for emphasis. "One, I know you saw her flinch when you took off your shades. Right?"

She nodded in agreement, a little afraid to encourage him. "Check. That was weird."

"Check." Bobby continued, raising a second finger to punctuate his list. "Two, she kept talking to you and never once made eye contact with me. And every time you looked back at her, she got really interested in her coffee."

Yes, that was true, too, albeit a little strange, so she nodded. "Check. Heavily into stirring. Gotcha." She laughed a little at the absurdity and continued to look at him, still a little puzzled. He was serious, so she motioned for him to continue.

"Okay, three. She didn't have to put that business in about hitting on other people's girlfriends, but she did. She made sure that we knew she was queer. I think that was intentional, and most likely for your benefit. Certainly not for mine."

Desperately wanting to argue, but noting that he was correct again, she agreed, reluctantly. "Check, again. Self-outing behaviors." As much as she really didn't want to know what was coming next, she encouraged him to continue, feeling a little as if she was watching a train wreck. "Go on."

He obliged, again ticking off the point with his fingers. "Four, I know I saw her cruising your tits at least once—"

"Hey," she interrupted, starting to get defensive. "She was definitely not 'cruising my tits,' as you so eloquently put it. That's just your horny guy spin on the situation."

He smiled back. "Well, granted, that may be true, but she was definitely looking at you. Besides, my particular horny guy spin on anything never includes the cruising of tits. Not my thing. Besides, there's more."

"More?" She was beginning to get exasperated with him.

Bobby pressed on. "Five, she shook your hand for at least twice as long as she shook mine."

She smiled, finally being offered something to refute. "I think she was afraid of you. You're kind of imposing, you know."

He nodded in agreement. "I know that, but the hand-shaking thing was still there. She digs you, Terri, and you're just all about the case."

She was quickly becoming aware of the fact that all of his observations had been correct so far. "Well, that is why we're here," she said in an attempt to steer the conversation back to firmer ground.

"Sweetie, I know why we're here. I think you should call her back and let her know that we're pretty sure she's got nothing to worry about. Also, if she really is withholding, you might find out what's going on better without me. I think you were right about her being afraid of me."

Terri allowed her memory to wander back to the quirky professor, with her coffee stirring and her sweet little dog. "Yeah, I guess she was kind of cute. Maybe I could do that."

"Fuckin' A right you could do that. Then you can ask her out to dinner, and take her into town for a little naked hotel-trashing."

"God, Bobby, you're such a pig, but, at least you're consistent." She let him stew on that for a moment. "I don't think so. She's work, Bobby, and you know how I feel about that. It's just not a good idea. And I still think that there's something she's not telling us."

He shook his head and stared back at her, a little deflated. "Okay, you know what's best for you. But I still think you're missing the boat here."

"Well, maybe, but it's better that way. No complications and no one gets hurt." Terri mustered up a smile. "Besides, naked hotel-trashing is your specialty, not mine."

Jen paced around her house. She was agitated. She had freaked and not told the FBI about Brad. "What the fuck was I thinking?" she talked to herself, pacing and fuming. Remote in hand, she scanned the channel guide looking for something mind-numbing that might keep her occupied long enough to calm down and figure out what to do.

Michigan. Jen hadn't thought about the events from Michigan in a long time. "And now they're back with a vengeance. Shit." Jen was seriously agitated.

She needed to call Joe. On the first attempt, she got his voicemail. "Joe, dude…it's me. You know—Jen." She rolled her eyes. "Never mind. Call me. Bye." She snapped her phone closed.

Before she ever got it back in her pocket, the phone started to vibrate. Caller ID showed her that it was Joe.

"Joe, I'm so glad you called. She was here. You know—my fantasy lesbian that's supposed to fall from the sky. Well, I don't know for sure that she's queer, but come on. Joe—"

"Jen, calm down. Tell me the whole story, this time from the beginning," said Joe.

"Terri. Her name was Terri. You should see her. She's a cop."

Joe sounded hesitant. "Um, Jen, honey, why was there a cop at your house?"

"Oh, that. Actually there were two of them, the FBI that is, and they had some questions about some people who do that same consulting thing that I do. You know, up there in Northern Virginia?"

"Yeah, Jen, I know." Joe was starting to sound impatient. "What happened?"

"Okay. From the beginning." Jen flopped down on the leather sofa. "I got a phone call from the feds yesterday, they came out to talk to me today."

Jen could hear the anticipation in Joe's voice. "Well, did you hit on her?"

"No. Duh, she was all about the work. Besides, she was here with this huge guy. I was afraid he'd, like, judo chop me or something."

"I don't think they really do that, do they?"

"No, probably not, but he was pretty intimidating. Anyway, I guess there's something going on with NoVaGenEx. Some employees have been killed, and the feds are trying to find a connection. They asked me all those questions you hear on TV. Do you have any enemies? Anyone you pissed off in your past? All that kind of stuff."

"The big question, Jen. Did you tell them about that hacker guy from Michigan? You know, the one from that weird computer shop."

Brad. There he was again. She stopped. Flashes of memory of a very naïve college student who thought she had the world by the tail popped into her head along with the results of some of the stupid decisions she had made while she was still that kid. She shook them off. "No. I mean, he was just a jerk who hit on me. I didn't even know what he was up to. It wasn't that big a deal, anyway. Besides, he's still in prison for, like, five more years. You think I should have told them about him?"

"Yes, you spaz, you should have. I know you'd like to forget about the whole incident, but he wasn't just a jerk who hit on you. He was your hacker buddy and you're the reason the cops even found him. You also testified against him, and he got put away for a long time, but not forever. You didn't see the way he looked at you when they took him out of the courtroom. He was creepy, and you don't know for sure that he's still in the big house."

"What?" She paused, trying to process exactly what he had just said. "Joe, did you just say big house?"

"Yeah, too many gangster movies. But anyway, you need to tell them about him. What if he's out and still pissed off or something? This could be bad, Jen, very bad."

"That's not going to happen. It's so clichéd. Besides, you've seen *Fatal Attraction* too many times. Ms. All-big-and-bad-and-buttoned-up just distracted me and I wanted to be all, you know, cool. Not like she looked twice at me anyhow. I could call her. They said that they'd still be in town for a while."

"Call her now, Jen. This freaks me out, and I'm three thousand miles away. I know Cujo Junior, Spawn of Satan is there to protect you, but if this guy's out and looking for you…"

Jen knew he was probably right. "I know, I know. I'll call her right now."

She heard his audible sigh of relief. "Okay, I feel better now. Did you forget anything else?"

She shook her head. "No, I don't think so."

"Glorious tits?"

God, he just never stopped. "Shit, Joe, I didn't even look." She paused to think, remembering the hot babe with the sunglasses. "Well, actually, I did look a little, but I couldn't tell. She had on a suit jacket that covered everything."

"See, Jen, one more reason to give her a call. I need to know about these things."

Jen finally relented, said her good-byes, and went to her office to get the number to call the FBI.

❖

A call to the office had turned up no new information on either the case or Jennifer Rosenberg. Terri sat at a table in a local sandwich shop typing notes into her PDA and watching Bobby wolf down a sandwich. When her phone rang, Terri assumed it would be the office with even more unhelpful information, but the caller ID told her otherwise. She flipped open the phone and spoke, "Agent McKinnon."

The voice on the other end of the call was hesitant. "Um, hi, Agent McKinnon, this is Jennifer Rosenberg, you know, from earlier."

"Yes, ma'am, I do remember. Is there something I can do for you?" Terri mouthed "Rosenberg" to Bobby across the table. He shrugged back at her. Terri held up one finger to indicate that he should wait.

The hesitation was still there. "Well, um, there's this thing, you know, I kind of forgot about. I may have more information for you." Nervous pause. "Can we talk again?"

"More information?" Bobby began gesturing wildly at Terri, pointing at the phone and acting like a mime pretending to drink something. "Hold on a second, please. Agent Kraft has a question." She covered the phone and asked, "What the hell are you doing?"

"She has more information, and you could meet her at the hotel bar next door to get it. Ask her to come for a drink. How much information can she have?"

Jesus, he was so pushy. "Bobby, shut up. This is business." She pointed right at him and whispered, "And see, I told you she was keeping something from us." She put the phone back to her ear and calmly slipped back into agent mode. "Dr. Rosenberg, I appreciate the call. Will you be available at home for the next couple of hours?"

She heard the nervous pause again. "Well, Agent McKinnon, I could recommend somewhere nice for, maybe, I don't know, dinner? We could talk then."

"Just a moment, ma'am." Terri covered the phone again. "Bobby, I think she just asked me out to dinner. Holy shit!"

Bobby looked astonished, but then broke into a wide smile. "Holy shit is right. I told you she wanted you. Say yes, fool!"

Terri took a deep breath to steady herself, as well as to remind herself that this was business and that Jennifer Rosenberg was part of the job. Nothing more. "Thank you, Dr. Rosenberg, that's a most generous offer, but I'll have to decline. Agent Kraft and I will be out to your place in an hour or two."

Jen continued on the other end of the call, definitely sounding a little deflated. "There's just one thing, if you don't mind me asking. Could you please stop with the 'Dr. Rosenberg' and all the 'yes ma'am' and 'no ma'am'? It's a little weird for me. Everyone else calls me Jennifer or just Jen. Could you try that?"

"Sure, um, Jen." Bobby mouthed "Jen" and gave Terri a

hearty two thumbs up. Terri shook her head and waved him off. "I'll see you in a couple hours. Thanks for calling."

Terri looked at the phone once before closing it, then looked up at Bobby. He was squirming in his seat. People were starting to stare. "Girl, I told you."

Terri pulled at the arm of Bobby's jacket to get him out of crazy person mode, but she had to laugh at his antics. "God, Bobby, you're such a goof. Besides, whatever you think is going on with her, isn't. Trust me. We're working here."

"Yes, Agent McKinnon, I know that. Understood. I just thought you deserved a little fun too."

Terri knew he was thinking of her. He always did. Best friends want you to be happy, but this was not the way. Work made her happy. That was all she really needed.

"Bobby…work…remember? Now, let's go. It's getting late and I'm thinking hotel for the night. Gives us a place to work. I want to check my e-mail before we go out there again, and you have calls to make."

CHAPTER NINE

Terri stood in front of the mirror in her hotel room, smoothing her jacket, when she heard a knock. Bobby stepped into the room when she opened the door. "Well, not my first choice, but if it's all you've got. You can't go wrong with jeans and a black turtleneck."

"Shut up, Bobby." She turned away from him, adjusted her black leather jacket again, and asked, "Can you see my sidearm?"

"Nope, it's all good."

Terri took a deep breath and got back to business. "Now, are you coming along, or are you staying here to make phone calls?

Bobby grinned. "I think you can handle one cute little lesbian all by yourself. You are armed, after all."

Terri looked around the top of the dresser for something to throw at him.

He shrugged. "I have to say it. It's what I do. I'll hang here and check in if you think you've got Dr. Rosenberg under control."

She stared at him, looking for a smile, a twinkle in his eye, or anything else that looked like more teasing. "Works for me," she said and headed out, leaving Bobby standing alone in her room. "Lock the door on your way out."

He leaned out of the door and called after her, "I won't wait up." Without even turning around, Terri raised her right hand over her head, calmly flipped him off, and continued down the hallway toward the stairs.

❖

Jen checked the full-length mirror in the bedroom one last time. "Not bad, eh, Snickers?" He didn't have anything to say, but continued to stare at her. "Well, I think I look hot." She really did, decked out in a jade green turtleneck, black jeans, and black suede boots. "God, I hope the ol' gaydar isn't busted, or else all this hotness is just going to waste." She headed downstairs to wait for Agent McKinnon. A knock at the door stopped her halfway to the kitchen. Jen smiled, turned around, and pulled the door open.

"Agent McKinnon. Welcome back." Jen stood back to allow Terri through the door. "Wow, you look really different." Jen studied her a little closer. "I guess it's your hair."

Terri idly fidgeted with the loose ends of her hair. "Well, it's technically the weekend, so I don't have to keep it up off my collar."

"I must say it suits you. Not so, what's the word, agenty?"

Terri smiled. "I suppose the word 'regulation' might be better, but 'agenty' works too."

Jen motioned toward the kitchen. "Can I get you some coffee?"

"Um, sure, that would be great." Terri leaned down to pet Snickers, who was wagging his tail furiously. "He sure is friendly, isn't he?"

Jen reached for mugs and peered at her dog. "Not usually, no, but he seems to like you. Have a seat."

Terri seated herself at the kitchen table in the same chair she had used during her first visit to the farmhouse. "Now, you said you had some information for me."

Jen suddenly felt stupid. Somehow she had let Joe convince her that she should explain this completely embarrassing situation from her college days to a federal agent. "You know, I'm pretty sure it's nothing, but Agent Kraft did say something about spurned suitors, and I got to thinking, and then my friend Joe called, and he thought I should tell you, but I'm sure it's nothing. After all, the guy is still in prison."

"Your friend is in prison?"

Jen felt really stupid. "No, I'm sorry." She felt heat rise to her cheeks. "Okay, here it is. This is embarrassing. I used to know this guy in Ann Arbor. Creepy little guy, but you could tell he was always up to something, always thinking. He'd get this funny look in his eyes, but I was nineteen. What did I know?" Jen shrugged. "Anyway, I found out that he was a computer geek like me, and we started hanging out a lot. I thought he was going to help me get into MIT. He was amazing when it came to programming. He helped me with my classes, let me bounce project ideas off him, told me I was brilliant, stuff like that." Jen blushed and lowered her head. "I was so busy learning computer stuff from him I didn't notice that he was into some seriously advanced cryptology stuff. One time, I asked him what he was doing and he told me that he was hacking into a bank over in Detroit."

Terri arched her eyebrows. "Not messing around, was he?"

"Um, no, he wasn't. But I thought it was cool. You know, nineteen years old, thought I wouldn't get caught."

"Caught? Caught doing what?"

"Helping him. Showing him new ways to get around firewalls that we talked about in class, stuff like that." Jen felt really small. "Evidently, he managed to hack into the Bank of America."

Agent McKinnon remained silent. Jen wasn't sure what she was thinking, but it made her nervous. "I was walking home one night, and these two guys in suits followed me across the quad to the burger joint where I liked to stop. Before I got to the door, they pulled me around the side of a building, showed me their cool little wallet things that proved they were the FBI, and asked me what I knew about Brad Davis. Scared the shit out of me."

"I'm sure it did." Agent McKinnon was still cool as a cucumber. That made Jen even more nervous. "What did they do?"

"Well, it dragged out for a couple of days, but they eventually made me a deal." Jen shrugged. "In exchange for my testimony, they'd let me go. I'm sure the mega mogul lawyer that my dad showed up with helped, but they let me go scot-free."

Jen hesitated and looked at Terri, who smiled and set her PDA down. "Well, Dr. Rosen...Jen, I really appreciate you telling me about this. I don't know—"

"There's more."

"I'm sorry for interrupting. Go on."

"No problem. Anyway, he ended up getting convicted and sent to prison. I went to grad school after that and never really thought about him again until now. My friend Joe thought I should tell you mostly because Joe always worries about me. He always thought Brad was creepy."

"And did you? Think he was creepy, I mean?"

"Well, yeah. He smoked too much and never had any friends. He spent all of his time with his computers instead of people. And he always looked at me funny. Showed up places where I was having drinks with friends, stuff like that."

Terri leaned forward in her chair. "He was stalking you?"

Jen considered that for a moment. "Well, I never looked at it like that. He said he wanted to work with me on some programming projects he had lined up. I was kind of flattered."

"So, a man you didn't know tracked your activities enough to know how you spent your out-of-class time, asked you about projects you were working on in class in order to get close to you. You eventually went to work with him, involving yourself in a federal crime, and later testified against him, resulting in his being sent to prison?"

"When you say it, it sounds so bad."

Agent McKinnon arched her eyebrow and stood. "Dr.— Jen, here's what I'm going to do. I'm going to take this information that you have given me. There isn't anything else is there?"

Jen shook her head.

"Okay, I'm going to take this to my office and make a few phone calls. I don't want you to worry. I'm sure this Davis guy is still in prison, but I'll make some inquiries. In the meantime, you go on about your business, but hang on to my number in case you think of anything else."

Jen rose and walked Terri to the door with Snickers trailing at their heels. They shook hands and Jen watched until the big black SUV was out of sight. "Well, Snick, that wasn't quite the romantic seduction I had hoped it would be, was it?"

❖

Terri was barely back on the main road toward town when she called Bobby.

"Hey there, Agent McKinnon, how are things down on the farm?"

"A little more complicated than either of us thought, I'm afraid. It seems that Dr. Rosenberg has a bit of a past that includes pissing off a computer hacker and getting him sent to prison."

Bobby whistled. "Wow, it's always the quiet ones, isn't it? What do you want to do?"

"I'll be back at the hotel in about fifteen minutes. Why don't you call DC and check this out? Maybe it's nothing. Maybe Bradley Davis is still in prison, but I have a funny feeling about this one, Bobby."

"It's never good when your Spidey-sense lights up, Terri. Never."

CHAPTER TEN

Terri sat at her desk, head in one hand and elbow on the desk while she fiddled with her pen and stared into space. It was Monday, it was raining, and she was trapped in a dreary, nondescript office waiting for the phone to ring. She looked at her notes for what seemed like the hundredth time, hoping for some new revelation, but none was forthcoming. She continued to wait, trying not to stare at the phone. Her research from earlier that morning had led to some of the details of the case that Jen had left out. Bradley Allen Davis, also known as Alan Davis, a cyber thief who had slipped up and been caught by a college kid because he thought he was smarter than she was, had evidently made some threats against that college kid. She had not been informed about the threats because he had made them on the way to the maximum security prison where he had been incarcerated ever since. At least Terri hoped that he was still incarcerated. Regardless of her denials to Bobby's teasing, she liked Jen Rosenberg. She was funny, quirky, and everything Terri was not, and she most definitely did not deserve to be harassed by an ex-con with an ax to grind. Bobby came back into the office with two cups of coffee and some paperwork under his arm "Anything from the Great White North?"

"Not a peep. They must be out ice fishing or something. Did you get the faxes about this Davis creep?"

Bobby had e-mailed both the Ann Arbor and Detroit police departments requesting information about the case. He held up two folders for her to see and tossed them onto her desk. "There's not much there that we don't already know. Your Dr. Rosenberg apparently told you most of it."

"She's not my Dr. Rosenberg." Terri shook her head. "Oh, never mind. You said most of it. What else is there?"

"Did she mention that she was offered immunity for her testimony?"

Terri closed the folder slowly and looked up at Bobby. "She was involved in the hacking? I find that hard to believe. She's so...so..."

"Innocent?" Bobby gave her his best "oh, please, girl" look. "Come on, Terri, you know as well as I do that you can't judge a book by its rainbow cover. According to the lead investigator, she was believed to have played a minor role in Davis's operation, but they had no hard evidence. Sounds to me like they scared the crap out of a young girl to get what they wanted."

"Damn," Terri responded. She didn't know what to think. If Jen had been involved, it certainly would make her a target for Davis—if he was even out. But what about the other victims? What was their connection to Davis?

She tossed the folders back across the desk when the phone on Bobby's desk rang. "Agent Kraft," he said. Terri focused intently on Bobby's end of the conversation. He listened, asked to clarify a date, wrote a name and phone number on his pad, thanked the voice on the other end, and hung up the phone. Terri looked Bobby in the eye, his next words putting voice to what she had been fearing the most.

"He's out."

❖

Bradley Allen Davis, who until recently was simply known as Terre Haute Federal Correctional Complex Inmate Number 50301, awoke with a start as a passing fire truck broke the silence of his slumber. Maybe silence wasn't the right word. His new apartment was on one of the busiest streets in town, which meant his bedroom window was less than ten yards from the 24/7 stream of traffic along Jackson Avenue.

"Fuck!" Bradley tried to shake off the anger that had smoldered constantly in his head since his incarceration ten years earlier. The early release from his fifteen-year sentence had been welcome, but sometimes he was unsure. There was a certain level of comfort to the prison routine, and the constant fear of physical abuse had actually become comfortable as well. His mom always used to tell him, "You get used to hanging if you hang long enough." Well, he knew all about hanging now. The daily harassment could be counted on, even scheduled if he really stopped to think about it. At least the prison didn't sound the horn to open the cells for breakfast before six a.m. From his mattress on the floor he looked over at the clock on the milk crate.

"Four o'clock in the morning…what the fuck? Can't a guy even be allowed to sleep through the night?" He spoke to no one in particular, which was good since no one else was in the apartment. He contemplated lying back down to try to sleep but knew it would be futile. There was far too much on his mind, and way too many things to do. His freedom was hardly that. There were visits to the parole officer downtown, visits to the doctor to try to find the cause of the blinding headaches that plagued him almost daily, and the constant harassment of phone calls from these and all of the other random idiots that he had to deal with every day.

His incarceration at Terre Haute Federal Prison was based on charges relating to an extensive list of cyber crimes. Bradley Allen Davis had been the man to call if you wanted to steal something from someone via the Internet. Questionable shady "businessmen" in downtown Detroit had often found his skills in separating someone from his money a better option than physical harm, and Bradley was good at it.

His nondescript looks drew little attention. There was nothing memorable about his appearance, and he intended to keep it that way. Out of sight, out of mind. He was smart, but according to the Federal Bureau of Prisons, not smart enough to keep his ass out of prison. Well, Bradley knew better, and it was just a matter of time and patience before he could prove it to those stupid fuckers.

He got up from the makeshift bed and shuffled barefoot into the tiny galley kitchen. His one concession to cooking of any kind was the coffee maker that was constantly bubbling to keep the caffeine flowing to his ever-busy brain. The soul-sucking quacks that claimed to practice medicine at the University Hospital suggested that maybe his headaches were somehow linked to the constant flow of caffeine into his body, but they could all just soundly kiss his ass if they thought he was going to stop for them. They suggested that his three-pack-a-day cigarette habit might contribute as well, but that wasn't going to stop anytime soon, either.

He contemplated these issues as he shook the coffee grounds from the bag into the filter on the well-worn, formerly white Mr. Coffee next to the sink. Once the water was added and the coffee was started, he flipped open the lid on the box of Marlboros, pulled one free with his teeth, and leaned over the gas burner on his battered stove to spark the butt to life. Dragging heavily on the cigarette, he felt the first morning rush of nicotine and began to shake off his anger at being awakened by the fire engine. Maybe if he could just convince those idiots at the hospital that the headaches had more to do with the daily beatings he received at Terre Haute than any small issues with either caffeine or nicotine, he just might be able to get some relief. The small flow of Percocet from the hospital helped a little. So did the small baggies of marijuana that the skater punk with the weird haircut seemed to never run out of, but Bradley Allen Davis knew resolutely that there was only one true cure for the almost constant pain in his head.

Revenge. Find the little bitch who had landed him in prison. Scare the shit out of her. Then end her pathetic existence. Take her life away just like she had taken his. Jennifer Rosenberg— her name made his head ache. She would never see it coming. The plan was beautiful—just complicated enough to keep the cops guessing but with a poetic twist that he would be happy to point out to *Dr.* Rosenberg just before he blew her brains out. Dr. Rosenberg. She had always thought she was smarter than he was, but he would show her and everyone else who had ever underestimated him exactly how smart he was. His plan was foolproof.

Rosenberg had been difficult to find, but not impossible. She might have been a better hacker than he was, but he could still show her a thing or two. Being the sanctimonious little bitch that she was, she had helped the cops find him rather than risk her ass. The last taste of freedom that he'd been allowed to enjoy before his incarceration was shattered violently as a team of heavily armed FBI agents broke down the door to his apartment, yanked him from the office chair at his state-of-the-art computer system, threw him to the floor, and told him that he had the right to remain silent.

And he'd done exactly that. Remained silent. About his activities and his clients. Unfortunately, his clients were equally silent, especially when it came time to post bail, so he didn't see the proverbial light of day until his release from Terre Haute almost ten years later. Fortunately for him, he knew enough from his own illegal activities to realize that banks were no place to keep your money. The strongbox buried under the shed in his mother's backyard was his choice for squirreling away large sums of cash. He had spent ten years hoping that no one had found his stash of over a quarter of a million dollars. It had to be enough to get him through the end of his plan. The plan that was already in motion.

Chapter Eleven

Terri stood by the window of her fifth-floor office in the Hoover Building. It was Wednesday, and it was still raining. Washington was depressing in the rain.

"Have you talked to her yet?" asked Bobby.

She turned away from the gray and depressing view outside her window to the institutional, fluorescent-lit, equally depressing view inside the window. "I've been trying since we heard about Davis. I only get her voicemail, and this is definitely something I don't want to leave on voicemail."

Bobby seated himself at his desk and waved her over. "Yeah, I get that. You should deliver this news yourself…or I can always do it if you're feeling too close."

Terri heard exactly what he was driving at, but she had been careful not to get too close. Yes, she liked Jennifer Rosenberg, but in the way that you like someone for their outlook on life or the way they laugh at a joke, not in a personal way, not in a relationship way. She wasn't going down that road again, regardless of how attractive she found Jen to be.

"No, I'm fine. Do you have anything new?" She gestured toward the files on his desk and pulled out a crime scene photo.

"Nope. We've got three crimes that, with the exception of

the random number generator thing, don't seem to have any other connections. According to NoVaGenEx, the vics weren't even working on the same project. We have an ex-con who appears to be a model parolee, which means we've got squat because we've got no one else. There are a half a dozen agents in at least four different cities, doing the same shit that we are, and they're coming up with exactly the same thing we are, which, by the way, is again squat." Bobby sounded frustrated. "Frankly, I'm not sure what our next move is other than to wait and see what happens. And I know how much you love to wait for things to happen."

Terri snorted. "No shit. So now we have to sit and wait for this sick bastard to kill someone else and hope he gives us the magic number. Asshole." She set down the photo and reached across the desk to pick up the NoVaGenEx file. "Bobby, do you think—"

"Agent McKinnon? You have a visitor."

Terri looked up and saw Jen step out from behind one of the building's escorts, wave sheepishly, and hold up her visitor badge. She took a deep breath and straightened her jacket.

"Thanks, Jim." Terri acknowledged the escort, who turned and left the office. "Hello, Dr. Rosenberg, what can we do for you?" Jen's smile dimmed a bit and Terri winced inwardly.

Bobby stood and motioned Jen over, then offered her his chair. "Here you go. It's nice to see you again, Dr. Rosenberg. I'll just go get us some coffee, and you and Terri can talk about what brings you here."

Once Bobby was out of earshot, Terri asked, "So, what does bring you here? Is everything all right? I've been trying to reach you."

Jen fiddled with her visitor badge. "I'm okay. I had to drive up to Herndon for a meeting at NoVaGenEx. I saw that you had called, but you didn't leave a message. I thought I would come by and see if maybe you'd like to have lunch."

Terri felt her chest get tight. She couldn't help but notice how great Jen looked in her navy blue pinstriped suit. "Um, I don't know that—"

A twenty dollar bill appeared over Jen's head. "Lunch is a great idea," Bobby said. "I'm swamped here or I'd join you, but bring me something back from the hot dog cart on the corner, would you?"

❖

Terri silently cursed Bobby during the elevator ride to the lobby.

"He's not nearly as scary as I thought," said Jen.

"Who? Bobby?" Terri laughed. "No, he's just big. He always teases me that I'm the badass cop in this partnership." She felt suddenly shy and needed to look at the floor. What was it about Jennifer Rosenberg that made Terri want to tell her all this stuff?

"That I'd like to see. You playing bad cop while Agent Big and Intimidating plays good cop. Oh look, it stopped raining."

Terri had completely forgotten about the rain. The sky was still leaden and threatening as they walked down the block to the hot dog cart.

"Is this okay?" she asked. "If he doesn't get fed every few hours, he gets cranky."

Jen laughed at that. Her nose crinkled and one dimple formed on her left cheek. Terri found it hard to pull her attention away from that dimple and its proximity to the turned-up corner of Jen's mouth.

"Sure it's okay," Jen responded. "I like a hot dog as much as the next gal. Now, are you going to tell me why you called me and didn't leave a message?"

Terri placed their order with the street vendor and paid before she said anything else. She debated how to say what she had to say, but in the end, the direct approach seemed best. "I have to tell you I'm really glad you showed up today because I didn't want to say this over the phone. Davis is out of prison."

Jen's expression quickly changed to a look of abject terror. The smile was gone; the dimple receded, replaced by worry lines and a furrowed brow. "Oh shit," she breathed.

Terri took Jen by the elbow and steered her to a nearby bench. "Listen, that came out worse than I meant it. Yes, he is out of prison, but I spoke with his parole officer. He got out right before Christmas for good behavior. He had been a model prisoner, evidently, and since his crime was nonviolent he earned an early release. While he's been out, he's never missed or even been late to see his parole officer, and he's monitored regularly. He has a job at his apartment complex up there in Ann Arbor. Granted, it isn't much of a job, but it provides him with a place to live. He sees a doctor regularly, and he's never missed an appointment."

"Doctor?"

"He has some kind of chronic condition that requires regular medical care. I don't know what. That's a doctor-patient confidentiality issue, but the point is his parole officer assured me that he couldn't be our guy."

"Really? He can't?"

"No, Jen, I don't see how. I just wanted to be able to tell you because I was afraid that you'd be worried."

"Well, I was worried." Jen looked really concerned. "Are you sure?"

"Yes, we're sure." Terri clenched her fists to keep from touching Jen's hand. Just to comfort her, of course.

Jen brightened a little, which made Terri feel unreasonably happy. "Thanks for that." Jen really did look relieved. "So, what does that mean for you folks? You and Bobby, that is."

Terri really hadn't thought that far ahead. "Well, since there's no evidence against Davis and no connection between the crimes that we can figure out, the only choice we have right now is to wait."

The look on Jen's face was back to flirty smile. "So, let me ask you this, Agent McKinnon. Are you up for a celebratory dinner? A thank-God-my-computer-overlord-slash-stalker-is-not-out-to-get-me dinner? I mean, this is all good news, right? I'll be up here for the rest of the week going to meetings in Herndon, but Friday night we could maybe have dinner."

"I'd like that." The words were out of her mouth before Terri could pull them back. It was only dinner, and they *did* have something to celebrate. After dinner they could both go back to their normal lives. Somehow that was not the most comforting idea.

❖

Terri returned to her office after walking Jen to the Metro station. She dropped the bag containing Bobby's hot dogs on his desk.

"I could have sworn that hot dog cart was on the corner. What did you two do? Go to Anacostia for these?" Bobby asked.

"No, sorry, we were talking. Do you want me to get you new ones?"

"Of course not. What's wrong? You told her about Davis?"

Terri nodded and sat at her desk. "Yeah, I told her, and really it's good news. I'm just distracted."

"Because you like her and you were worried. Am I right?"

He was right and she was struggling with feelings that she had no idea how to deal with. Terri was definitely attracted to Jen Rosenberg. She also knew that acting on her attraction would end up being a mistake, but saying no was getting more and more difficult. "Hey, Bobby." Terri tossed a paper clip across the desk at his head.

"Ow! What?"

She leaned closer, whispering across the top of her desk. "I don't want to talk about this here. What's up tonight? Have you got plans?"

He thought for a second. "Nothing that the TiVo can't take care of."

"How about if you drive me home and I'll make you dinner?"

Bobby checked his watch, then stood and started to pack up his computer. "Sure, sounds great. We could knock off early. We put in overtime last weekend, and since you brought me an inedible lunch, you owe me. Grab your stuff, let's go."

❖

Terri had changed into her sweats and was busy at the counter chopping mushrooms, garlic, and onions for the pasta. Bobby sat on the stool next to the counter playing with the label on his beer. His coat and tie had been discarded and were now hanging on the back of a chair in the breakfast nook. Terri appreciated his patience, knowing it was killing him not to ask her about Jen.

"You said you needed to talk. What's up?"

She stopped chopping and poked around the pile of mushrooms on the cutting board with the tip of her knife. "I'm not sure what I'm doing."

"Looks to me like you're making little mushrooms out of big ones."

Terri laughed softly. "Well, maybe mountains out of molehills. This is new stuff for me."

"What, chopping vegetables?"

She waved the knife at him. "Don't be a goof. You know damn well I'm not talking about vegetables."

Bobby threw his hands up in mock fear of the blade. "Easy, killer. Just giving you a little shit. My guess is that Dr. Rosenberg has thrown you for a loop. It was all just fine and dandy as long as she was part of the case because you could put her in a box where you didn't have to deal with her, but now that it looks like there might not be a case, you have a decision or two to make about the professor. How's that?"

She nodded. "Yeah, score one for the big guy."

"Oh, and let's not forget all of the angst and blame that you're still carrying around about Alyssa."

Terri nodded and remained silent. Bobby took a giant swig from his beer and set it on the counter. "Yeah, I thought so. Anyway, let's start with Dr. Rosenberg. You had lunch with her today and?"

"And it was really nice. Once we got past the whole Davis is out of prison thing, we just walked and talked. She's here in meetings until Friday and she asked me to dinner Friday night."

"Well, all right, Terri! This is good news."

She wished she felt the same way. "I don't know, Bobby. These things are always so easy for you, but all I can see is potential disaster. We have dinner, we talk, we flirt, and then what? She lives two hours away. She has a completely different life, and you know as well as I do that long-term relationships and the Bureau don't mix." Bobby started to say something, but Terri stopped him. "And if you say one word about getting laid, I'm going to beat you to death with a spatula."

"Noted," Bobby answered with a grin. "Terri, you're going to have to help me out here. You are so far down the road with this and you don't need to be. Jennifer Rosenberg is a nice gal, a college professor. Can't you just have dinner with the woman without all this introspective torture?"

Terri was exasperated at her own inability to figure things out. "Oh, God, Bobby, I don't know. My life has always been simple. The work stuff and the personal stuff never cross paths—I've made sure of that—but now there's Jen. I mean, we've had one lunch. That's hardly enough to plan a future together, now is it? But I feel like there could be something there. I don't know."

"Well, I've heard tales about you lesbians and your U-Hauls."

She considered throwing an empty tomato can at him. "No U-Haul here, but my track record is not good, and it's just easier to live without the complication."

"Sweetie, your track record is fucked, but it's not your fault. What happened to Alyssa was terrible, but there was nothing you could do."

"I know, Bobby, but come on. This is the first time in, well, since Alyssa died that I've actually thought about opening up to someone new. And you know as well as I do that the inside of my head can be a scary place at times." Bobby nodded. "I just don't want to scare her off, and despite whatever noise you make to the contrary, I'm not sure I'm ready."

"So, why did you agree to have dinner with her?"

She smiled. "Because I like her."

"So you like her. There's nothing wrong with that."

"All things being normal, I'd say there was nothing wrong with it. But you know I just can't seem to get a handle on normal."

"Ah, normal's overrated. Besides, considering what we do for a living, I think it would be a waste not to grab on to this. I know the case makes it way more complicated than if you had met her at the library or wherever it is you meet girls, but, Terri, you have to see this through."

"You really think so?"

"Yeah, sweetie, I do. Not like I'm the shining example anyone should choose as to how to live their life, but I do know that love—"

"Who said anything about love?"

"Whoa, easy there, big fella." He backed off, raising his hands. "What I mean is that love, affection, real human contact, define it how you will, is just not that easy to come by." He dropped his hands and took a swallow of beer. "Casual sex, that's easy. Real connections to other people…that's not easy, and it's rare and wonderful. Why not want that? It's a good thing."

Terri chuckled. "Why, thank you, Martha Stewart." She couldn't decide whether she wanted to smack him or hug him. Probably both. "And thank you, Bobby."

"Anytime." Bobby crossed his arms over his chest and asked, "Now, are we going to eat soon or what? The big guy is famished."

CHAPTER TWELVE

Jen was running late, but it couldn't be helped. Her manager had been late, so of course the meeting had taken twice as long as it should have. To add insult to injury, she was now sitting on the parking lot that was officially known as eastbound I-66 on Friday afternoon at five thirty. Jen called Terri from her 4Runner to bitch about her plight and apologize, but Terri's calm voice soothed Jen's fragile nerves. Terri assured her that she could use the extra time to get ready and that they'd head out to dinner as soon as she arrived.

Jen sat back in the driver's seat, turned up the radio, and looked over to the flowers in the passenger seat, silently wondering if they were too much. She decided that it was a sweet and romantic gesture and definitely not too much. She also wondered if it was prudent not to have a disaster plan. "Shake it off, Rosenberg. One step at a time."

The traffic finally started to move, while Jen started to calm down. It only took forty-five minutes to get to Dupont Circle. Terri's neighborhood had a completely different feel from the hectic, traffic-filled hustle and bustle just a block away. Terri's row house stood with its neighbors, three stories of whitewashed brick, decorative wrought iron bars protecting the windows and ivy trailing up the stairs to the front door.

Quiet and elegant, just like its owner. Jen whistled. "Nice digs, Agent McKinnon." Remembering to bring the flowers, she locked the car, bounded up the steps, and rang the doorbell. She heard feet pounding down the stairs inside, then slower steps approaching the door. The inside door swung open revealing the beautiful Agent McKinnon. Jen smiled as Terri crossed the small space to the outer door and opened it, inviting Jen into her home.

"These are for you." Jen felt strangely shy as she held out the flowers. "I hope it's not too much."

Terri smiled. "No, they're perfect." She looked at the flowers and back to Jen. "Thank you. You can leave your case over there next to mine." She motioned to the chair by the door. "Come on back to the kitchen, and I'll find something to put these in."

Jen dropped off her laptop and moved to follow toward the back of the house, but stopped when she spotted a small black and white cat peeking out from under the sofa in the living room. "Hey, you must be Jojo."

As she bent to pet the cat, Terri called from the kitchen, "Since you're wearing black pants, don't let her near your ankles. She's a fur bomb."

Jen laughed and scratched Jojo's head. "No worries, we're okay here, aren't we, Jojo?" The cat purred and tried to lean against Jen's legs, forcing her to jump up and back, effectively avoiding the determined little beast. "No way, puss. I've got your number." Laughter in the kitchen reminded her of why she was here, so she stepped around the cat and followed the musical sound through the dining room and into the back of the house.

Leaning against the kitchen door frame with her hands in her pockets, Jen availed herself of the time to check out

Terri as she added water to a large glass vase. "All-business" Agent McKinnon of the black suit and sunglasses had been replaced by a softly casual girl Jen was finding it hard not to stare at. A navy blue wool jacket covered a crisp white blouse that revealed the merest hint of cleavage. While Terri arranged the flowers in the vase, Jen's glance drifted downward to her long, floaty floral print skirt, finally coming to rest on the navy blue clogs that completed the outfit. Jen smiled at the choice of comfy footwear. How could this woman be so completely sexy without even trying?

Terri turned, setting the flowers in their vase on the counter, and said, "Wow, you look nice."

Jen blushed. "Thanks. I was just thinking the same thing about you."

"Thank you." Terri blushed a little too and bit her lower lip. After a moment, she looked up and asked, "Ready to go? I'm hungry."

"Sure, where we going?"

"Do you like Thai?"

❖

Terri held the door to the Thai Café and ushered Jen through with a hand on the small of her back. Bobby had suggested this particular restaurant because it was Terri's favorite place to stop for carryout on the way home. "Home field advantage, Agent McKinnon," he had said. To Terri, that sounded like a good idea. She was nervous enough about going to dinner with Jen, so not having to worry about the food was good.

Jen looked radiant in her green silk blouse. Terri noticed that it did lovely things to highlight the color of her eyes. She looked again when Jen leaned over to brush the last crumbs of someone else's dinner from her chair. Black corduroy slacks hugged her butt in just the right way. Terri caught herself staring.

"Do you come here very often?" Jen asked.

Terri evidently had been staring a bit too intently, because the question surprised her. "What? Oh, yeah, once in a while." Jen was smiling while she dropped her napkin in her lap. There was that dimple again. "Usually just to pick up something to take home." Terri's face got hot.

"So, what's good? I'll eat anything." A funny look crossed Jen's face. "Well, not *anything* anything, you know, but, pretty much anything."

"I've only had the yellow curry, so—"

"Only the yellow curry?" Jen looked over her menu and teased, "What's wrong, Agent McKinnon, afraid of the pad Thai?"

"No, I'm not afraid of the…oh wait." She saw the smile on Jen's face and knew immediately that she was kidding. "I get it. Sorry, I'm a little slow on the uptake sometimes. Especially when I'm nervous." Oops. There it was again, Terri telling all of her secrets to Jen Rosenberg. Why was she doing that?

"Now, why are you nervous?" Jen's face showed nothing but concern, while she closed her menu and set it on the table. "Are you afraid of me, Agent McKinnon?"

"No." Terri was adamant. "I'm not afraid of you. I just haven't done this for a long time."

"Done what? Gone out to eat?" Jen teased.

Terri sat back to give the waiter room to put two glasses of water on the table. "Are you ladies ready to order?"

Terri silently thanked the waiter for giving her a second to breathe. Despite insisting to Jen that she wasn't afraid of her, Terri really was and she didn't understand why. Maybe it had something to do with the way Jen was looking at her. There was something there, something Terri couldn't quite figure out.

"I'll have the pad Thai, extra peanuts, please," Jen ordered with a bright smile for the waiter.

"Yes, ma'am." He turned his attention toward Terri. "And you want yellow curry with pork?"

Terri flushed bright red. "Yes, please." Jen covered her mouth with her hand, Terri assumed to keep from laughing. "Thank you."

The waiter nodded and turned to leave, but Jen stopped him. "Hang on." She turned toward Terri. "Do you want to get a bottle of wine?"

"Sure, that would be nice. Whatever you like is fine." Terri really wasn't much of a drinker, but it was starting to sound like a good idea.

Jen perused the wine list. "Ooh, that sounds yummy." She pointed to the menu and looked up at the waiter. "This one."

"Afton Mountain Gewürztraminer. I'll be right back with that." He turned and left.

Jen turned her attention back toward Terri. "Now, we were talking about you. What haven't you done for a long time?"

"Gone out on a date with someone—well, someone that Bobby didn't set me up with." Terri felt strangely shy again. She fiddled with her napkin and stared at the candle on the table. After a moment she looked up. Jen was smiling.

"Is this a date, Agent McKinnon?"

"You did bring me flowers."

"Yes, I did."

"And you don't have to call me Agent McKinnon, you know."

Jen smiled.

"I like calling you that. Makes me feel special." Jen lightly bit her lower lip. "Like I have my own personal g-man to take care of me."

God, she was cute. Terri felt like her head was on fire. "That's sweet." She took a drink of water, and added, "But considering my track record, you might not think that's a good thing." Shit. There it was again. She was going to tell Jen everything. Why was this happening?

Jen leaned forward, elbows on the table. "What's wrong with your track record?"

Somehow, Terri knew that she needed to tell Jen the whole story, so she took another drink. "Five years ago. Late April. It was raining and Bobby and I were walking down Twenty-second toward P Street." Jen nodded for her to continue. "We were supposed to meet Alyssa, the girl I had been going out with for a while, at Apex. It's a dance club Bobby likes to go to." Jen nodded again, but held up a hand for Terri to wait while the waiter delivered the wine. He poured them each a glass and set the bottle on the table.

"Thank you." Jen smiled at the waiter and motioned for Terri to continue her story. "Please."

Terri took a healthy sip of her wine. "It's good." Jen nodded her agreement. "Anyway, Alyssa worked in a real estate office over in that same part of town. I used to worry about her walking home alone just because that isn't a nice area. There's a little park spot with lots of gang activity, robberies, stuff like that, but she swore that she was fine. I wanted to meet her at her office, but Bobby and I got held up in a meeting, so I called her to have her meet us at the bar." Terri stopped to get another drink. It was starting to warm her insides and calm her down. Good. "So we were walking around toward the edge of the park, and Bobby spotted Alyssa, but there was a kid there with her. He looked fifteen, maybe sixteen, kind of jumpy like a tweaker. I thought he was just talking to her, you know, trying to panhandle some cash, but then I saw the barrel of his gun when the light caught it." Terri closed her eyes and saw it again. "His hand was shaking. He was as scared as she was. Then I got scared because a nervous kid, armed and hopped up on meth, is a really dangerous thing."

Jen nodded. "I'd say that's an understatement."

"I've been accused of having that gift."

"Somehow, that doesn't surprise me. But we're getting off track. Finish your story."

Terri took another swig of wine. "Right. Anyway, Alyssa must have seen us, and she started to cry. She was terrified."

"Sure she was." Jen was leaning on the table again.

"The kid freaked. He pulled the trigger, and she went down. I didn't know how bad or anything. I told Bobby to check on her, and I took off after the kid when he bolted."

Jen didn't look amused anymore. She looked horrified. "Oh, God, Terri. What happened?"

"I chased him all the way back up to Twenty-second and he tried to duck up an alley to lose me. It was a dead end. I yanked him off a fence and came very close to—" She hesitated. "Well, I almost killed him. Bobby had to pull me off."

"Bobby?" Jen looked confused. "I thought he was checking on your friend."

"He was." Terri wasn't sure she could get through this next part. She fortified herself with one more slug of wine. "He checked on her long enough to see that it was too late to help her. He called for backup and came running after me." Terri looked down and picked at something on the tablecloth. "I couldn't protect her. That's my job and I couldn't keep it from happening." Terri swallowed her fear and looked Jen in the eye. "So you see, Dr. Rosenberg, if you're looking for a bodyguard, I'm probably not your best choice."

Jen looked downright shocked. "What? Are you kidding? Oops—" She sat back to give the waiter room to set down her pad Thai. "Yay, extra peanuts. Thank you." She looked across to Terri's plate. "Ooh, that looks good."

Terri looked at her own yellow curry. It looked just like it always did in the white paper carton at home, teeming with basil and pineapple. "Smells good," she said and picked up her chopsticks. Her first slice of pork wasn't all the way to her mouth when Jen started talking again.

"Okay, first thing." Jen gestured with her own chopsticks while she talked. "I'm not looking for a bodyguard." She sat up and defiantly stuck out her jaw. "I can take care of myself."

Terri didn't doubt that. "I bet you can."

"Of course I can. And am I to understand that you blame yourself for what happened?"

Terri nodded. It wasn't polite to talk with your mouth full.

"Sounds like a heinous twist of fate to me. What could you have done?" Jen looked genuinely perplexed.

Terri shrugged. "Nothing, really. And the worst part is that I know that."

"But you loved her and you couldn't fix it, right?"

"Very astute, Dr. Rosenberg." Terri raised her glass. "To protect and serve. That's what we do, and I couldn't protect her."

"And now you live like a monk and talk to your cat because you've decided that you're never going to get hurt like that again?"

"Yes."

Jen shook her head and set down her chopsticks. Terri was a little surprised when she reached across the table to take her by the hand. "That's such a waste."

"A waste? What?"

"Just that, a waste. You're so attractive, you're obviously smart, and you're hiding from something. Yourself maybe."

Terri really liked the way Jen's hand felt. Warm and soft. But Terri could also feel strength. "So maybe that's true." She looked into Jen's eyes and found more strength there. "Maybe it's time for me to stop hiding, take a chance."

Jen brightened and squeezed Terri's hand. "I could help you with that."

Terri felt shy again. "I didn't scare you off?"

"Psssht. It takes a lot more than a tough lady cop with a soft, whipped chocolate center to scare me off. Remember, I can take care of myself."

Terri knew, as Jen used her chopsticks to feed Terri a bite of pad Thai, that she would do anything to keep her safe. Jen held her mouth open, begging for a taste of yellow curry. Terri decided right then and there that Jen was also the cutest thing that she had ever seen. Ever.

❖

Terri stepped out of the restaurant to where Jen was waiting for her on the sidewalk. Jen patted her stomach and complained, "I ate too much."

"We could walk over toward the bookstore." Terri pointed across the street. "Lambda Rising is right over there."

"Marvelous plan, Agent McKinnon." Jen took Terri by the hand. Despite the chill of the evening, Terri felt her face get hot again. "You know, I've lived down there in the weeds for, wow, it's close to four years now." Jen motioned around with her free hand. "I've never come up here just to look around. All the rainbow flags make me happy."

"It is nice," Terri said. "I love it here. It's really different from home. Southwestern Ohio isn't exactly resplendent with rainbows and pink triangles."

"I would imagine not, but I've never been there," Jen teased while she pulled Terri across Connecticut Avenue. "Will you take me there, show me around? Give me a ride on your tractor?"

Terri laughed and stopped on the corner. "You know something, Dr. Rosenberg?" Jen was forced to turn back to see what was going on. "I think I'd take you anywhere you wanted to go." Terri felt shy again. She stared at the sidewalk while Jen came close and took her by both hands.

"You're so cute." Jen nuzzled up close and whispered, "But you're the one who wanted to go to the bookstore." Terri felt momentarily deflated when Jen pulled her along.

Less than a block later, Terri was holding the door, ushering Jen through. Jen seemed happy as she looked around the shelves. "Like a kid in a candy store," Terri muttered to herself.

They laughed at the cards in the back of the store, and worked their way forward past the mysteries and into the best sellers. Terri lost track of Jen for just a second, but quickly spotted her toward the front of the store. Jen must have thought she was momentarily alone as she pulled a collection of lesbian erotica from a shelf and began thumbing through the pages. Not as alone as she thought. Terri couldn't stand it. She approached as quietly as she could and put her hands on Jen's hips from behind. She whispered, "Don't buy that one. I already have it and you can borrow it if you want."

Jen jumped, realizing she'd been busted, and quickly

launched into a tirade of self-defense. "I-I-I was just looking... you know, me with the being interested in what's selling these days and all..."

Terri tossed her head back and laughed. "Hey, I already 'fessed up to owning it. You could at least admit to wanting to read it."

"Well, okay, I was thinking about getting it. But, hey, don't have to, right?" She put the book back on the shelf.

"Right...So did you see anything else here," Terri motioned around the room, "that you want to take home?"

Jen rubbed her chin and attempted to look like she was lost in deep thought. "Well, there is this really hot FBI agent..."

Terri felt her insides flip and her knees turn to jelly. She was a goner. "Dr. Rosenberg, you truly are a flirt."

They walked the last block holding hands. The night was cold enough to explain why they huddled so close as they walked back to Terri's house. They were just inside the door when Terri suggested coffee, then added, "I might even have some dessert in the freezer."

"That sounds nice," Jen said as she pondered her next move. Walking up quietly as Terri added water to the coffeepot in the sink, she placed her hands on Terri's hips, mimicking the actions from earlier in the bookstore, and whispered, "Or we could just skip it."

Terri melted into the words. She turned around, still in Jen's grasp. She lifted her hands to Jen's face and pulled her in close. Their lips met softly, tentatively at first, then desire took over, elevating the kiss to mind-blowing proportions.

As she felt Jen's hands wandering lower, pulling her in closer, Terri felt something hard grind into her thigh. Jen, close to breathless, broke the kiss and quipped, "Why, Agent McKinnon, is that a pistol in your skirt or are you just happy to—" Realization dawned in her computer-professor brain and her eyes opened wide in shock as she stepped back. "Holy shit, that really is a pistol in your skirt."

The situation seemed so absurd that Terri could only laugh. "Yes, that is a pistol in my skirt, but I *am* happy to see you, if that makes you feel better."

She was relieved to see that Jen was laughing too, shaking her head and calming from her outburst before saying, "I guess I've still got some things to get used to here."

Terri took Jen's hands and held them. "Not too much, is it?" Memories of Alyssa's hatred of firearms popped into Terri's head. She was becoming concerned and knew that it showed on her face. She could also see the concern on Jen's face, and watched as it softened to an expression of gentle resolve.

Jen took a deep breath. "No, no, it's fine. Really." Terri closed her eyes as Jen placed a gentle kiss on first her right hand, then her left. "I guess it's finally time for me to make good on all of those hot lady cop fantasies I've been having for all these years." Jen released Terri's hands and pinned Terri against the counter with a hand on either side of her hips.

The kiss resumed, free from any discussions of anxiety or concealed weapons. Terri stopped to breathe and rub her cheek lightly against Jen's face, like a cat marking its scent. She whispered, more like a breath than actual words, "You have hot lady cop fantasies? I think I'd like to hear about that."

She felt Jen melt at the request. She was like so much pudding in Terri's arms, head rolling to the side as Terri kissed all the way down and back up her neck. Jen groaned, "Mmm… God, that feels good…you don't have a nightstick, do you?"

Terri stopped kissing and buried her face in Jen's shoulder, laughing. Looking up into sparkling green eyes, she asked a question that she already knew the answer to. "Jen, you're kind of a nut, aren't you?"

"Well, Agent McKinnon, you're the investigator." She undid one button on Terri's blouse and looked up in mock surprise. "What do you think?" Another button. "Hmmm?" She traced a line with her index finger from Terri's chin, down through the path of newly exposed skin.

"I think, Dr. Rosenberg, that you can't possibly expect"— she gasped audibly as Jen's mouth replaced her finger, gently retracing the path with small, wet kisses—"me to answer that question…mmm…that's nice…if you keep distracting me."

"I'm" *kiss* "not" *kiss* "trying to" *kiss* "distract you."

"Well, it's remarkably…ahh…effective." Terri took a deep breath in an attempt to restrain her reactions, but Jen was now on a mission. She pressed her body forward, pinning Terri up against the counter. Terri held her hands out, urging Jen to slow down. "I don't suppose I could distract you long enough"—she looked up—"to take this somewhere, um, a little more comfortable?"

An innocent smile played out across Jen's face. "Are you suggesting, I don't know, maybe your bedroom?"

Terri teased a little, answering in a light singsong tone, "There's more cop stuff up there."

"Oh, God…Really?" Jen squeaked.

"Mm-hmm."

Jen was the one to take the calming breath this time. "Care to show me?"

Without another word, Terri took Jen by the hand and led her from the kitchen, through the house, and up the stairs. They stopped at the first door so Terri could point out the bathroom, but then she quickly pulled Jen through the last door, the one that led to her bedroom. Jen stopped in her tracks, taking in the details of the room. "Ooh, you have a fireplace. Can you light it?"

Terri left her standing by the bed to approach the fireplace and turn a knob. She watched as the fire sparked to life. "Better?"

"Well, not yet." Jen pouted a little. Terri looked at her quizzically. Jen answered, "You're over there and I'm over here."

Terri walked over and wrapped her arms around Jen, pulling her close. "See, that was easy to fix." Terri kissed her again, and it was slow and wonderful, while she unbuttoned and removed Jen's blouse. Terri took Jen by the wrists, slowing her movements. "Just hold that thought for a second. I have to take care of something."

Jen watched, rapt, as Terri stepped back and pulled her skirt up, revealing her SIG Sauer P-228. Terri removed it from the holster, released the clip, and pulled back the slide to clear the chamber. She took off the thigh holster and turned to put everything in its place in the top drawer of her dresser. Turning back to face Jen, who was in the process of staring, slightly glassy-eyed, she asked, "Jen, are you okay?"

"Wow, this whole hot lady cop fantasy thing is worse than I thought." She sat down hard on the edge of the bed, shaking her head in amazement, imitating the motion of pulling back the slide as she spoke. "I mean, you were all like, um, with the thing, and...*woof*...damn!" Jen kept trying to speak, her mouth opening and closing like a fish, but nothing came out.

Terri came back to the bed, kicked off her shoes, hiked her skirt up, and straddled Jen's lap. Taking Jen's face in her hands again, she whispered, "I'm a little afraid your head will explode if I tell you that there are handcuffs in that drawer too."

The resultant reaction actually surprised Terri. She felt insistent hands roughly grab the open sides of her blouse, yanking her over onto the bed hard enough to make her yelp with surprise. Whatever Terri originally had in mind was dismissed, as all plans for slow, gentle exploration were lost to a certain college professor's vivid imaginings of law enforcement paraphernalia. She tossed her shirt and bra over the side of the bed. Jen smiled and followed suit. Their breathing came hard and fast as their excitement grew.

"Jen?"

"Yeah?"

"Take off my skirt?"

"Mmm, sure." Jen rolled over onto her side, undid the button and zipper, and removed the skirt with one quick pull. Terri watched the determination in Jen's eyes as she removed her own shoes, socks, and pants, adding more discarded clothing to the pile. Jen attempted to return to her perch on top, but Terri grabbed her by the wrists, and with a quick push-pull combination, landed Jen flat on her back with her hands now pinned over her head. She was wearing nothing but black satin panties and a glazed look in her eyes. Terri returned the look with an evil grin and waggle of her eyebrows, lowering her body to pin Jen to the bed. She dropped her head to Jen's neck, kissing slowly from the ear to the shoulder and back, grazing at the midpoint with her teeth. A low voice in her ear growled, "Please, Terri, do that," so Terri bit down, hard. Jen hissed and arched her back, grinding her crotch into Terri's thigh, breathing hard and demanding more. Terri obliged, biting hard enough to leave marks on Jen's pale neck. "Yes, like that…oh, God, Terri…"

Jen whimpered slightly when Terri released her hands, but moaned again when Terri told her, "Keep them there." Terri watched Jen grab the covers of the bed with both hands in order to do as she was told, arching her body as Terri trailed kisses past her collarbone toward her right breast. Reaching her destination, Terri first kissed and then licked one nipple, then lightly pinched and twisted the other one. She moved forward, using her thigh to apply pressure between Jen's legs, feeling Jen's body tense as though it just might explode. Not yet, though, as Terri ceased her ministrations and got up, pulling at the waist of Jen's underwear.

Terri took off her own underwear and returned, supporting her upper body with her hands and using her hips to spread Jen's legs, grinding her pelvis against Jen's exposed wetness. She felt Jen's legs wrap around her ass, urging her forward, and she reveled in the new sensations that the position allowed. Terri could sense Jen struggling to hang on to the covers and watched as her hands opened and closed. "Terri, please…"

"What?"

Jen was begging. "I need to touch you."

"What do you need to touch?"

Jen panted out her request. "I need to feel your breasts."

Rather than fully allow this, Terri decided to help. She leaned forward, teasing Jen's face with the breasts she'd begged to touch. Jen captured a nipple in her mouth and sucked. Terri felt her nipple grow hard, and she arched her back, groaning. She whimpered as Jen gave the nipple one last long lick, and she shuddered as she lowered her head and felt the caress of warm breath on her ear. "You do have glorious tits."

Terri dropped her head to the shoulder below her and laughed between ragged breaths. "Thank you." She arched again as Jen managed to scoot under her enough to capture the heretofore unattended breast with her teeth, lightly biting down, sparking the hot-wire connection between nipple and clit. Knowing that she'd fulfilled the request, Terri slid back down and shifted, supporting herself on her elbow. Using light strokes, she traced a path down Jen's sternum, trailing out and around Jen's small breasts, drawing out a moan. After a liberal amount of teasing, she watched, fascinated, as she trailed her hand down toward soft curls. Terri stopped just long enough to make eye contact, silently asking for permission before she reached down to stroke Jen's opening. Terri groaned as her fingers touched soft lips for the first time. "Oh my God, you're so fucking wet." Terri knew that her words sent lightning bolts straight to Jen's clit when she heard the moan and felt the hips pressing forward toward the fingers playing around her opening.

Frustration drove Jen to speak. "God, Terri, I need you."

"What do you need?"

"I need more of you."

"Tell me, Jen." She leaned closer, her mouth almost touching Jen's ear, and lowered her voice. "Tell me exactly what you need."

"I need you...oh, shit," she panted, the power of speech beginning to elude her as the maddening touch continued. "I need you to fuck me...please..." In a growl, she demanded, "Now."

Terri obliged, entering Jen firmly with two fingers. Jen bucked her hips up, attempting to deepen the contact. "More... please...more," she gasped between the slow, steady thrusts. Terri got on her knees and supported her upper body with an extended left arm. She withdrew, added a third finger, and entered again, harder and faster than the first time. Jen's eyes went wide; she threw her head back and opened her mouth in a silent cry of satisfaction. Each thrust was met with an upward motion of her hips, lifting her ass from the bed. Terri hadn't even touched her clit, but she knew that the first rumblings of climax were beginning in Jen's gut as she begged to be fucked even harder. Grabbing at the covers hard enough to pull the fitted sheet from the mattress, Jen cried out, announcing loudly that she was about to come. Three more deep thrusts and she was arching fully off the bed, crying out with a throaty sound that could only be described as primal. Terri slowed both the speed and intensity of her thrusts as vaginal muscles clamped down, compressing her fingers almost painfully. She rode out Jen's orgasm, letting her body tell Terri what she needed to know. Finally, stopping the motions altogether but leaving her fingers inside, she lowered herself again to cover Jen with her own body, pressing her into the mattress.

As she slowly emerged from her incoherent state, Jen lazily waved a hand in front of her face and finally spoke. "Oh, wow...stars." After she regained the ability to focus, she looked into Terri's eyes. "Jesus, that was, oof, that was amazing." She let her arm fall bonelessly back to the bed. "Damn, Terri, they teach you that at FBI school?"

Terri smiled. "Once again, that is of my own design." She wiggled her fingers inside, making Jen toss her head back, gasp, and buck one last time.

"Agent McKinnon, you need to stop that. I could just... explode." She motioned up and out with her hands. "Boom."

Terri reluctantly removed her fingers. Rolling to the left, she fell onto her back with her hands over her head. She turned her head to look at Jen, still lost in her just-been-fucked stupor. Jen raised her hand, extending her index finger, and said, "I'll be right with you."

"Take your time." Terri laughed softly, more than a little satisfied with the puddle of goo that the other body on the bed next to her had been reduced to. "I'm not going anywhere."

When she was finally able to move, Jen sat up, pulled Terri over by her arm, and rolled over her, landing hard in a sitting position on the bed, effectively switching places. Terri laughed as Jen explained, "Sorry, I'm right-handed. Doesn't work the other way."

"Well," Terri continued to laugh, "that little maneuver was certainly slick."

"I would venture a guess," Jen said as she traced a line

with her fingernails down Terri's overheated body, "that I don't have a monopoly on slick around here." Terri gasped as Jen's fingers found the wetness between her legs. "Nope, not me… you've got plenty of slick going on here." Jen continued to play with Terri's opening, teasing up to find her clit, and began lightly rubbing it in small circles. She tested with various angles and pressures, checking for intensity of reaction. The teasing was maddening for Terri. Finally moved to the point of frustration, she reached up and grabbed Jen's upper arms, pulled her closer to make full eye contact, and said, "I need you to stop doing that."

"What?" Jen replied with mock innocence as she discovered another particularly effective motion. "What am I doing?"

"Research…oh, God…you're doing…ahh…um… research."

"Well, what should I be doing?"

"I think…mmm…that you should"—gasp—"that you should quit goofing around and just fuck me."

Jen smiled and slid down to kneel between Terri's legs. "Like this?" Terri lifted her hips, reveling in the sensation as she was entered hard with two fingers. Needing to deepen the contact, she raised her hands up over her head, scattering pillows and flattening her palms against the bookcase headboard to apply counterpressure against Jen's insistent thrusting. Her back arched, lifting her pelvis to meet each stroke, and she groaned loudly as she felt the addition of a third finger.

She felt Jen lower her head to press an ear against her belly, wrapping an arm around her waist at the same time in an attempt to anchor herself more fully to Terri as she bucked and writhed. It didn't take long, between the three fingers in her and the thumb that contacted her clit with each stroke, before Terri was calling out, mostly using the word "yes" punctuated by a small assortment of expletives. She suddenly stopped moving and stiffened as her orgasm rose quickly from her toes and exploded in her groin, blacking out her vision, forcing a growl from her throat. Arching one last time, fully removing everything but her shoulders and the bottoms of her feet from the bed, Terri landed with a grunt as Jen slowed her movements and slid up to kiss her neck. Terri removed her hands from the headboard and twined her fingers through the messy hair of the head that was now resting on her chest.

As Terri returned to earth, Jen raised her head and asked, "Are you okay?"

"Oh, yeah, I'm…I'm just great. I can't feel my toes, but other than that…"

"Terri, that was amazing."

"You said that before."

"Yeah, but I didn't get to watch before." Jen wiggled her fingers, still buried deep inside her. Terri jumped a little and then relaxed as the fingers were slowly withdrawn. She let out a little whimper of protest, missing the contact, but watched intently as Jen studied the still-wet fingers of her right hand before raising them to her mouth, sucking the juice from them one by one. She then wiggled the fingers, holding them out for Terri to see. "Look…pruney."

Terri laughed. "Jen, you *are* a nut."

"Yeah, well, I didn't hear you complaining about that a couple of minutes ago." Jen rolled over to rest on her back, smiling.

"Oh, I'm certainly not complaining. I'm just thinking that…" Terri rolled onto her side and propped herself up on her elbow. "I could get used to it."

Jen rolled her head to meet Terri's gaze. "Oh, yeah?"

"Yeah," Terri answered as she began tracing a line with her index finger, starting at Jen's chin and down her throat.

"Cool. Me too." Jen stopped the hand, grabbing it and pulling it to her mouth to kiss Terri's finger. "Definitely could get used to this." She held Terri's hand in both of her own, pulling in close for a snuggle.

"Jen?"

"Hmm?"

"Were you planning on staying here tonight?"

"Well, I kind of, you know, was hoping. But, hey, presume much?"

"You think maybe I could talk you into it?" Terri waggled her eyebrows.

Jen rubbed her chin, pretending to think. "I don't know… how exactly were you planning to do that?"

"Well…" Terri rolled on top of Jen and kissed her throat. "I thought"…*kiss*… She moved lower. "That maybe" *kiss*… lower yet. "I might try" *kiss*…still moving. "Something like this."

As Terri reached her destination, she felt fingers weave into her hair, holding her head firmly, pulling her closer. Knowing that actions spoke louder than words, Terri used her mouth and tongue in new places to convince Jen to stay for the weekend. The only response she needed to hear was one very simple statement.

"I have…oh, my God…I have class on Monday."

CHAPTER THIRTEEN

Terri was the first one up. She pulled on a black tank top and flannel pajama bottoms before heading downstairs to finish making the pot of coffee that had been interrupted the night before. Halfway out the bedroom door, she remembered that Jen's luggage was still in the car, and also noticed that last night's pile of clothing had become a cat bed for Jojo, so she grabbed a pair of sweats and an oversized T-shirt just in case, leaving them on the foot of the bed. She also remembered to grab her cell phone off the nightstand for whenever Bobby decided to call. She did not want to wake Jen prematurely. Stealing one last glance at the decidedly cute college professor snoring lightly in her bed, Terri smiled, tucked the phone in her pocket, and went down to the kitchen.

She had just started to make coffee when, exactly as she expected, her cell phone went off. "Good morning, Bobby. Couldn't stand it for one more minute, could you?"

"Good morning, sunshine. Of course I couldn't stand it. I want dirt!"

"Well, you'll get none from me. Besides, I just got up and—"

"Just got up?" Bobby sounded incredulous. "Terri, in all

the years that I've known you, you've never made it past eight a.m. It's almost eleven now."

"Eleven?" Terri was a little embarrassed. "Really?" She checked the clock on the microwave to confirm. "I guess we were up kind of late." Smiling at the memory of the previous night's activities, she went to check the fridge to get some inspiration for breakfast. She came to the conclusion that it would be better to wait and just ask, and instead she got two mugs from the cabinet and waited for the coffee to finish as Bobby continued.

"So, any plans for today? Want to maybe hit the club tonight and see if that defective groove thing of yours is back in working order?"

Terri briefly entertained a thought about dancing with Jen. "I don't know. We don't have any official plans for the day. Maybe she'd like that."

"There you go. Why don't you just ask her?"

She thought again. "I could do that…actually she's not up yet, so…"

"Wow, she's not up yet? Terri, you dog, did you wear her out or something?"

"Bobby, again I remind you that you're a pig."

"Yes, but since I get avoidance via insult to my question, I'll take that as a yes."

"You would."

Bobby laughed. "Of course I would. I'm a pig, remember?"

"How could I forget? Now, I have to go. Don't want to neglect my guest. I'll call you later."

She took coffee up to Jen. Entering the bedroom, she could see that Jen hadn't moved an inch. "I really must have worn her out." Terri smiled as certain vivid details of her extremely late night resurfaced. She set the coffee down on the nightstand next to Jen's side of the bed.

As nice as the memories were, Terri wanted Jen awake since their time together was limited. She tried the gentle approach, smoothing Jen's hair and tracing the length of her nose with one finger. Jen lazily swatted at the hand like it was an errant mosquito, demonstrating that the gentle approach was probably futile. There was always the direct approach.

"Jen!"

Her eyes flew open, momentarily panicked, then relaxed when she saw Terri's smiling face.

"Oh, hey, it's you. Good morning." She rolled onto her back and stretched languorously, like a cat. "What time is it?"

"It's after eleven."

"Wow, really? You must have worn me out. I haven't slept that well in years." Jen sat up, pulling the sheets up to cover her naked torso. "Do I smell coffee?"

"Yep, two sugars, right?" Terri pointed to the mug on the nightstand.

"Yeah, that's right. How did you know that? Oh, wait. It's the agenty thing, isn't it? It's all in the details, right?"

"Well, yes, I do tend to notice people's little quirks more often than the average guy. Occupational hazard, I guess."

"So, Agent McKinnon, do you have plans for today? Any hot bad-guy action that might tear you away from me?" Jen blew on the coffee and took a small test sip.

Terri climbed back into bed, propping herself on the pillows to sit next to Jen. "Well, no, but good-guy action has been offered. Bobby called earlier. He wants to go dancing, and wanted us to—"

"You've already talked to him?" She couldn't help but laugh. "He just couldn't stand it, could he?"

"No, I'm afraid not. He's a little pushy that way. That doesn't bother you, does it?"

"No, of course not. I've already figured out that he's part of the whole Terri McKinnon package. Besides, I like that he worries about you." She took another sip of her coffee. "My buddy Joe is like that. He'll expect a full report on Monday. I hope that doesn't bother you."

"No, how could it? Our friends are our friends and I guess we're just lucky to have people who care about us like that."

Jen took another sip of the steaming brew and set the mug on the nightstand next to her. "Terri, there is one thing that's bothering me."

"What's that?"

"It's just that I'm naked and in bed with a smokin' hot, girl-type cop person and we're talking about men." She turned, swinging her right leg over to straddle Terri, and put her hands on Terri's collarbones. "Seems to me there are better things to talk about."

Terri played along. "Like what?"

"Like how amazing you look in that tank top comes screaming to mind."

Terri laughed. "Anything else?"

Jen tilted Terri's face up as if to kiss her, but stopped just short, looking Terri right in the eye. "Yes. It needs to come off."

Terri's last coherent thought as the clothing was peeled from her body was that Bobby was going to be waiting a long time for that return phone call.

❖

Hours passed and the light faded from the bedroom window, replaced by the dark chill of the early February evening. Terri sat stubbornly on the edge of the bed, watching as Jen begged, "C'mon, Terri, please."

Terri crossed her arms across her chest resolutely. "Why should I?"

"Because I agreed to go out dancing with your best friend. I feel like I'm auditioning. And besides, I'm really not some kind of control freak nutcase that's going to expect to do this all the time."

Terri still wasn't convinced. "I know, Jen, but…"

Jen offered a compromise. "Oh, hey, how about if I let you pick mine out? My luggage is right there." She pointed to her suitcase for emphasis. "Anything you want."

"Okay." Terri still wasn't convinced, but she softened a little more to the idea of allowing Jen to dress her for Funky Retro Night at the bar.

Jen just kept right on plugging away. "C'mon, it'll be fun. It's Eighties night. You won't look freaky at all." She paused, evidently considering her statement. "Well, maybe a little, but, hey, that's the point, right? Besides, you can pull it off. You've definitely got the arms for it. Not to mention that spectacular butt." Terri blushed. "You'll knock 'em dead."

"Jen, stop it." Knowing that she wasn't winning this one, Terri finally gave in. "I'll do it. But cargo pants and a tank top? Oh my God! I'm never going to hear the end of this from Bobby." She snatched the offending items of clothing from Jen's hands, shooting one last evil glance her way. Task completed, she modeled for Jen, stopping to check herself out in the full-length mirror on the back of the door. Jen spooned in behind her with hands on the hips of the black cargo pants.

"See, you look great. I told you. And also, you can put your gun in one of those big pockets on the side. No one will ever know."

Terri was finally convinced. "I guess I do look all right."

She continued to stare at her reflection. Something seemed familiar. "But, you know, something just struck me." Jen looked quizzically at Terri in the mirror. "How many times have you seen *Terminator 2*?"

It was Jen's turn to blush and look away, pretending to be really interested in the paint job on the bedroom wall. "Not that many, I-I-I don't know, maybe…"

"Jen…" Terri's tone was low and just slightly menacing.

Jen gave in. "Okay, twenty-three. I've seen *Terminator 2* twenty-three times. Happy now?"

Terri turned around to give Jen a hug. "Yes, I am happy now. Except you haven't even started getting dressed. Pick something out and hurry up, because Bobby will be here any second. I'll take a rain check on the selection process, but you owe me one."

As if on cue, the doorbell rang downstairs, signaling Bobby's arrival. "See, he's here. Get dressed and I'll feed him the rest of the pizza." She started out the door, but stopped to collect a slightly sloppy kiss, and then headed down the stairs to admit Bobby.

Terri hit the bottom of the steps and trotted to the front door, startling Jojo under the sofa in the process. She opened both doors to let Bobby in, and turned to show off her clothing before he had the chance to ask.

"She picked that out for you, didn't she?"

As she looked down at her outfit, Terri became slightly afraid of what might come next. "Yeah…why?"

"Oh, just because I know you'd never try that on your own. Sarah Connor, as I live and breathe."

"Oh, God. Not you too."

Bobby grinned and hugged her. "Terri, you look fabulous. Besides, you're practically glowing. Things are good?"

She smiled. "Yeah, things are good. Actually, things are so good it scares me a little."

He rolled his eyes. "I know, God forbid you should be happy, right?"

"No, Bobby, it's not that. I wish I could shake it, but I keep thinking about Davis…"

Bobby reached out to take Terri by her upper arms, attempting to assuage her fears. "Sweetie, it's okay. He's in Michigan, the picture of a reformed convict. We'll figure out the rest of it. We usually do. And if it turns out that Jen really is in any kind of danger, we'll figure that out too."

Terri thought about it for a second. "I know, I know… it'll be fine." She nodded, attempting to shake loose her fears. "Come on back to the kitchen and finish the pizza. Jen's still getting ready."

Bobby followed Terri back to the kitchen and helped himself to a beer from the refrigerator. He was halfway through his second slice when Jen appeared, decked in black jeans and boots, with an almost-tight red T-shirt and short black denim jacket. She greeted Bobby with a nod. "Agent Kraft."

"Please, just Bobby," he said through a partial mouthful of pizza. He wiped his hand on a kitchen towel and extended it to Jen. "Good to see you again. Better circumstances this time, though."

Jen shook his hand. "Yeah, definitely."

He hitched his thumb toward Terri, who was leaning against the stove, arms crossed over her chest, watching them interact. "I hear you're responsible for Agent McKinnon's daring new look here."

Jen laughed, and Terri was delighted to see them hitting it off so easily. "She was definitely not sure about it, but I think the results speak for themselves. Wouldn't you agree?"

"Absolutely. Very urban commando." He turned to wink at Terri and got up from his seat. "Now, you two, since I'm a slave to the beat, I think it's time to hit the road. Agreed?"

Jen and Terri nodded and murmured their agreement as they grabbed jackets to protect them from the chill of the February night. Once out on the sidewalk, Bobby said to Jen, "You know, she can do the one-handed shotgun pump thing just like in the movie." He mimicked the action. "I saw her do it once on the range when she thought I wasn't looking."

Jen looked up at him, her face turning red and her eyebrows practically crawling up to her scalp. "Really?" she squeaked.

Terri pointed at Bobby. "You stop it. I knew full well that you were looking when I did that. And you," she turned, pointing to Jen, "you need to calm down. We're going out in public and I don't need to deal with a catatonic college professor all night. C'mon, let's go."

Bobby nudged Jen. "Ooh, when did she get all top?"

"I never noticed that she wasn't. You think this is new?"

Bobby threw his head back and roared with laughter. Terri just kept walking, knowing they would follow, and thought to herself, *Oh, this is just fucking great. Now I've got two of them.*

CHAPTER FOURTEEN

The pounding in his head never stopped. Sometimes it was worse than others. Mostly it was just there, like an uncomfortable itch, the kind that couldn't be scratched. Still, he kept driving on through the night because there was work to be done. It was all so simple. A fifty-dollar bill slipped surreptitiously into the proper hand, a basic tweak to the call forwarding so that his home phone rang through to his cell phone, and an easy acquisition of a new state driver's license. Bradley had it all figured out, which proved again that the idiots who had ruined his life were all completely clueless.

The trip to the hardware store was easy as well. Just stick to the mom-and-pop establishments that never asked for stupid details like phone numbers or zip codes. Plus, the fact that these businesses always preferred a cash transaction to the use of credit cards kept things from ever becoming difficult. The hardest part was the rental car, but again, nothing was ever impossible.

Bradley had left the apartment complex under the cover of darkness, which in Michigan usually occurred somewhere between five and five thirty p.m. during the early weeks of February. The rental car, obtained with the use of false identification and stolen credit card numbers, allowed him to drive to his destination in absolute anonymity. Arriving close to midnight, he was shrouded in the darkness that rendered him invisible to the prying eyes of the daytime. Simple work to be done, should take no more than five minutes. Well, maybe ten, but that didn't matter.

He had everything he needed with him in the car. Coffee in the cup holder, three packs of Marlboros, a satellite map provided by the good folks at Google, and a flashlight. Oh, and his 9mm Glock, of course, silencer included. It was all he would need to continue the plan that would buy him his freedom. Freedom from the pain and the ghosts that continued to torture and humiliate him in his sleep every night.

After arriving at his destination in the city, he made two circles of the block to assess the working conditions. Quiet part of town, gaps in the lighting, loud animals kept indoors to protect them from the cold. Nothing he couldn't work with. He parked around the corner, slipped the Glock into the pocket of the black army surplus jacket that he always wore, closed the car door as gently as he could, and slipped from shadow to shadow until he arrived at his goal. He pulled latex gloves from inside his coat and slipped them on in preparation for doing what he had just driven six hours to accomplish.

The person he had come all that way to find was still up. A light in the window showed consultant number four hunched over his computer, just where Bradley figured he'd be. He crouched low to slip paper covers over his shoes before scuttling around the back fence, up past the shed, and onto the back porch. Once inside, he tiptoed, listening for sounds of activity in the office. Things were quiet save the tapping of keys on a computer. He leaned around the door and brought the Glock to bear. One squeeze of the trigger, and random consultant number four became victim number four. Bradley smiled. He rolled the body over to make his mark, and washed all of the blood from his gloves. One last study of the area with his flashlight, and Bradley left the way he came in, through the back door.

Six hours, one pair of latex gloves and paper shoe covers down the toilet of a rest area on the Ohio Turnpike, and one finished pack of smokes later, he dropped the car at the rental place and called a cab to take him home. He, of course, had the foresight to have the cab dump him several blocks from home, further clouding the trail from the potential eyes of the police. Arriving in his apartment after taking the circuitous route around the back of the Dumpsters, he noted the time. Six twenty-three a.m.

Mission accomplished.

CHAPTER FIFTEEN

Terri leaned on her desk, coffee in one hand, her head in the other, looking over old case files to finalize status. There was nothing new brewing, certainly nothing of the vengeful ex-con in Michigan variety. She heard the ding of the elevator and saw the doors slide open through the glass of the office wall. McNally was back from whatever meeting he had been to. She noticed the expression on his face was tense, with the edge of a sneer, but that wasn't really anything new. His stride always carried him purposefully in whatever direction he was going, but today the objective was his office. He didn't even look up to summon Terri and Bobby to his office, just barked out their last names and kept right on walking.

She heard the tone, recognized it as slightly gruffer than usual. Looking up, she caught Bobby's eyes, and could see that he had heard something different as well. She headed directly to the pit bull's office, followed closely by Bobby, who ushered her into the office and closed the door behind him. McNally pointed to the chairs facing him and dropped the files he'd been carrying onto the surface of his otherwise orderly desk. At the point where he would usually start barking monosyllabic instructions, Terri watched as something new transpired. McNally sat in his high-backed chair, tossed his glasses on the desk, and rubbed his face with both hands. Terri glanced at Bobby quickly to confirm that he too had seen McNally do something out of character, but Bobby's slight shrug indicated that he didn't know what it meant either. Terri thought that it couldn't possibly be good.

McNally finally provided the answer to their questions. "It's this NoVaGenEx thing. It just got worse." He pointed at the file on his desk. "One more NoVaGenEx computer consultant has been murdered. Bright red number seventeen on this one. I've just spent the last two hours upstairs convincing my boss that we've covered everything here, and there was nothing to lead us to anything that could have stopped this shit. But, hey now, along comes victim number four, same totally random number thing, but no suspect, no motive, nothing..." He stopped to make eye contact with Terri and Bobby. "But you two are going to fix that. The case is officially a serial murder and it's yours to run." He pushed the file across the desk toward Terri. "Look that over, make your calls, do that voodoo that you do, and give me a plan by the end of the day. Thank you."

Bobby ushered Terri out of the office ahead of him and turned to close the door. Terri walked slowly back to her desk.

"What's in there that's got him so riled up?" Bobby asked.

Terri took a deep breath to center herself. "Because we had to sit and wait, and now this sick bastard gives us victim number four, and I'd be willing to bet he hasn't given us another fucking thing. If he doesn't get cocky and screw up soon, I don't see how we can stop him."

"Oh, shit, you're right."

"Yeah, I'm right, but not for long. C'mon, let's get on the phone and find this guy before he does it again." She allowed herself to finish the thought in her head—*before he gets to Jen.*

Terri suggested that Bobby call the police in Pittsburgh while she called the parole officer in Ann Arbor to check on the status of Bradley Allen Davis.

"He hasn't gone anywhere." The parole officer was adamant. "He's checking in, made his clinic appointments at the hospital. He works every shift at his job." Terri heard papers shuffle on the other end of the call. "He did run some errands the other day, the drug store and things like that, but nothing out of the ordinary."

Terri shook her head. "Thank you." It wouldn't have been so bad if they had another suspect, but there was still nothing to tie Davis to anything. "Call us if anything changes." She hung up the phone.

Terri looked toward Bobby as he finished his call to Pittsburgh. She raised her eyebrows, silently asking if he'd discovered anything new. He just shook his head.

"Terri, we've got nothing new. The crime scene was as clean as the first three. Vic was shot through the back of the neck while he was working at his computer. The neighbors didn't hear a thing." Bobby threw his pen on the desk. "This is starting to really piss me off."

"I think that's the point," Terri said. Bobby cocked his head and stared at her. He looked confused. "Bobby, think about it. Whoever is doing this is setting something up."

"Yeah, now we just have to find out what that is." Bobby checked the report from the Pittsburgh Police. "Number seventeen. I'll call the crypto guys and let them know."

"Thanks. Not like I think it's going to get us anything."

"Why? What are you thinking now?"

"I think that these numbers mean something to someone besides the perp." Terri took a long breath and rubbed her eyes.

"Like he's trying to send a message to someone. A message that only this one person will understand."

Bobby sat up. "Okay, if that's his point, then how is he getting this info out to this mystery person, considering that we're keeping the number thing out of the public eye?"

"Maybe he wants us to deliver it." Terri shrugged. She was stabbing in the dark now, but it was all she had. "Maybe it's for someone that we've already talked to, or maybe he's going to deliver the message personally at some point in his diabolical plan."

"What?" Bobby laughed. "Did you just say 'diabolical plan'?"

"Yes." Terri waved him off. "Forget it. I'm just frustrated."

"I can see that. Terri, are you okay? You're more worked up than usual about this."

She let out a long breath. "Yeah, I'm fine. It's like putting together a jigsaw puzzle when all of the pieces are the same color. Great fun…if you're into frustration."

Bobby got up from his desk and came over to pull at the sleeve of her jacket. "Come on. Let's go downstairs and get a sandwich and take this discussion outside. We need to talk about some things and I don't think you'll want to be in the office for it."

Nodding, Terri idly thought that she was a little hungry and that sometimes a change of venue was good for the thought process. As the elevator doors closed, she turned to Bobby and asked, "Now what? We have another victim with no ties to anything or anyone but NoVaGenEx. There's no motive that I can see. None of these people were working on anything classified. They're all computer consultants like Jen, but they weren't working on a project with her. Maybe this has nothing to do with her, but I can't shake this feeling, Bobby. She's a part of this."

The elevator doors slid open to reveal another nondescript government hallway, but the sounds of a busy kitchen indicated the presence of the nearby cafeteria. Bobby motioned her forward and she ordered her food, then stood at the end of the line to wait as he loaded his tray. They paid quickly and headed for the terrace, where they could talk in relative privacy. Terri was glad for the uncharacteristically warm day. She had too much to say that she didn't want overheard inside the building. "Terri, what's going on up there?" he asked, pointing toward her head. "What do you mean Jen's a part of this?"

"Oh, I don't think she's in on it or anything. She couldn't be. There's nothing in the investigation to indicate she has had any contact with the victims. Quit looking at me like that. Of course I checked. I mean, I haven't checked on the vic from Pittsburgh, but she was with me all weekend."

Bobby shook his head, "You are awfully cool about this, Terri."

"I have to be, Bobby. It's the job, and now it's official and there's more stuff to process, and—"

"And?"

"And part of that stuff includes a list of potential victims that contains at least one name that's making this harder to process than usual."

"When did she go home?"

"Early Monday morning. She had class. Dammit, Bobby. This is what I get for taking your advice. I like her. She's amazingly smart, totally goofy—"

"Hot," he slipped in through another mouthful of sandwich.

Terri flushed and nodded. "That's not quite where I was

going with this, but yes, she's completely hot in this silly, quirky kind of way. I've never met anyone like her."

"Are you going to tell her about this latest development?"

"Well, Agent Kraft, now isn't that the million-dollar question?" She thought for a second before continuing. "We do have to inform the local jurisdictions around the consultant network that we officially suspect serial crimes here." Bobby nodded his assent. "I'm still not sure about how to deal with our list of potential victims. I mean, we have no evidence, no suspect, and I don't think it's in anyone's best interest to sound a general alarm. We might find something in the next few days that gives us a better idea of who the next victim might be."

"Yeah, I know the drill, but that still doesn't answer my question."

"Well, I guess that's because I don't have an answer to that question yet. No idea. This is one of those complicated issues I was trying to avoid. Guess it's too late now. Maybe I'll talk to her about it this weekend."

Bobby arched his eyebrows again, asking the silent question. Terri answered, "Yes, since it's a long weekend, she's coming up here again for a homemade dinner and some quiet movie watching. Come on. Let's go make those phone calls."

CHAPTER SIXTEEN

Jen could smell the scents of the dance floor. Sweat mingled with smoke, cologne, and spilled beer. She could feel the body behind her. Slightly sweaty, tight tank top, breasts pressed lightly into her back; well-muscled arms raised high overhead, dancing with abandon. She reached back, grabbing a pocket of the cargo pants, pulling the dancer closer, feeling Terri's pelvis lightly grind into her ass. God, that felt good. She allowed her own head to roll back, mouth open, savoring the delicious sensation all over her back as the lights flashed through her closed eyelids and the music drove them onward. She could feel the rumble of the tires…

Tires! "Oh, shit!" Jen felt the tires contact the rumble strips on the side of the highway, shaking her from the grip of the incredibly vivid memory. Pulling the wheel hard to the left to regain control, she silently thanked the Virginia Department of Transportation for the warning that kept her SUV from contacting the guardrail. "Rosenberg, get a grip. It's only one more hour." She shook her head and grabbed the travel mug in the cup holder between the front seats. Bracing herself with a long drink of her coffee, she released the last images of her night out at the bar with Terri and Bobby.

She spent a lot of time living in her own head with the

memories of the stunning Agent McKinnon, replaying every moment they had spent together since the day they met. Sure, they'd talked on the phone, a lot. Pretty much every day. There was even a flirty e-mail or two (or twelve). She'd also made good on her promise to share details with Joe. Well, not every detail. A girl had to keep something for herself, after all. She smiled a little and licked her lips in anticipation of what might transpire this weekend. Home-cooked meal, a glass or two of wine with dinner, maybe some ice cream, dripping into the cleavage between those glorious tits, straddling her lap as she licked it off…

"Rosenberg, stop! There's more going on here than that." There really was. Jen was a little confused by the whole thing. Not only did they talk on the phone, but Jen found herself counting the hours and minutes until the next time they talked. She caught herself wondering what Terri was doing during the times that they weren't on the phone. And it wasn't just about the sex. Jen missed seeing Terri when she wasn't around. So much it almost hurt.

"Oh, shit, Rosenberg," she warned her reflection in the rearview mirror. "You're falling and you're falling hard." The realization hit Jen like a ton of bricks.

Jen pulled into the driveway of the townhouse after a short battle through the Friday afternoon traffic of Connecticut Avenue. The front door opened and her own personal fantasy cop came bounding down the steps. Terri opened the car door and grabbed Jen by the shoulders as she stepped out, pulling her into an incredibly warm, wet kiss. Jen pulled Terri close by the belt loops of her jeans, leaning against the side of the car, reveling in the sensation of the body pushing her backward.

Oxygen becoming an issue, Jen pulled away to breathe and try to talk. "Wow, Agent McKinnon, you must be really glad to see me."

"Well, I think, judging by your reaction, that the feeling is mutual."

"Yeah, it is." Jen looked into Terri's eyes, tracing the line of her jaw with her finger. "How about you help me get my luggage into your lovely home, feed me something wonderful for dinner, and..." She waggled her eyebrows, pointedly not finishing the sentence.

"Why, Dr. Rosenberg, are you insinuating that I have lured you here for my own nefarious purpose?"

Jen laughed, raising her hands to show that her fingers were crossed. "Let's hope so!"

Several minutes later, following much kissing, fondling, and at least three more rounds of pin the lesbian to the wall, Jen was happily sitting on the kitchen counter with her first glass of wine. Not that it was somewhere she would normally choose to sit. She'd been picked up and placed there with an order to stay because Terri was concerned that dinner would be ruined if Jen couldn't keep her hands to herself, and it kept her out of the way. She was thoroughly enjoying the show as Terri busied herself around the kitchen, pulling a beef tenderloin and potatoes out of the oven, checking the broccoli in the steamer, and whipping up a simple vinaigrette for a spring green salad. Terri let the meat rest for a minute while she gathered plates from the cupboard over the sink. Jen had to duck to avoid the door, feeling like she was in the way, but all offers of assistance had been refused with a simple "Let me take care of you" from Terri.

Finally, after everything was settled, Jen was allowed down from her perch and led by the hand to the breakfast nook at the back of the kitchen. Dinner smelled great and she realized that she was really hungry, but she was stopped from digging in by a hand placed on her own. Terri raised her wineglass, offering a toast to comfort food and really great company. Terri asked her about the ride up.

"It was fine. No big deal." She left out the part about almost running off the road in a sweaty fantasy-induced haze and her realization that she was falling for Terri. "How about you? Any more bad-guy action?"

Terri shifted uncomfortably in her seat, took another long drink of her wine, and looked right at Jen. "Actually, there is something else that happened, and I've been debating about how to deal with it."

"Oh, yeah?"

"Yeah." Terri took a deep breath and continued, "I wasn't sure how to bring this up, or even if I should, but another of your coworkers was targeted and attacked earlier this week."

Jen was confused and a little surprised. "Why wouldn't you bring this up? Seems kind of important, I think."

"It might be and it might not. I didn't want to worry you needlessly, and there's not actually much to talk about." Jen wasn't sure how to read Terri's face. She seemed worried, but maybe a little guarded.

"Terri, is there something you're not telling me? 'Cause you seem a little, um, avoid-y. Like something's bothering you. If something big is going on here, please tell me. Maybe I can help."

Terri sat back down and took one more drink of the dark red Shiraz, evidently looking for a little alcohol-fueled courage to continue the conversation. "You see, Jen, the problem here is that the FBI has officially declared the case a serial murder. Bobby and I are heading up the investigation, so I'm a little torn here between what I should tell you, officially, and what

I want to tell you because I care so much about you. You're pretty important to me, if you haven't guessed that by now."

Jen was touched by Terri's kind thoughts, but was starting to get a little scared. "Terri, what are you talking about? How bad is this?" Actually, as she thought about it, she was leaving scared and heading into panicked. "Terri, is there something else going on here that you're not telling me?"

Terri set down her glass and pushed her untouched meal to the side. Leaning on the table, she took Jen's hands in hers and looked deep into her eyes, apparently both looking for and attempting to provide comfort and confidence. "Yes, someone else is dead. A consultant in Pittsburgh was murdered. Shot in the back of the neck."

As she felt herself start to shake, Jen gently pulled her hands free, picked up and drained her wineglass. She reached for the bottle and refilled her glass, draining more than half of it in one long slug. The wine began to warm her insides and calm the shakes. When she lowered the glass, she could see Terri watching her intently.

"I'm sorry, Terri. I'm not a lush or anything, really. It's just that—"

Terri stopped her with a finger to Jen's lips and smiled. "It's okay, Jen. I've seen plenty of people in tense situations, and watched them react in all kinds of ways. A shot of liquid courage is hardly uncommon." Terri took Jen's hands in hers. "The important thing here is, are you okay?"

"Actually, I'm not sure. Do you have any idea what this whole thing is about? Do you know who it might be? I mean, maybe it's a disgruntled employee or something like that."

Jen held tight to Terri's hands as she processed the rest of the thought. "Or do you think I'm in some kind of danger?"

"That's the problem. We don't have a clue. I have to be

honest with you, because you deserve that, but there's nothing. No motive, no suspects, no evidence. Nothing. So I can't answer your question." Terri looked away, appearing to be slightly ashamed, as a light dawned on Jen.

"Ah, that's what this is about. The avoidance, that is. Not that you didn't want to tell me, but that you don't know if you can help. Terri, I'm glad you told me, but I have to figure part of this out by myself. I know I kid around a lot and tease you about being all big and bad, and how you're going to keep me safe, but I can take care of myself. You don't have to be responsible for me." She reached for Terri's chin, tilting her face up to meet her gaze. "You know this doesn't change anything, right? I mean, I care a lot about you too, and I don't want you to worry about me." Terri nodded gently as Jen continued, "Besides, you could let me take care of you a little too, you know." She blinked hard to keep the tears she felt coming on at bay. "I may not have all the fancy handguns and stuff, but I'm smart and I have cunning and false bravado enough for both of us. Okay?"

Jen finally relaxed a little when Terri laughed and nodded, "I know you do. I just don't want to let you down."

"Terri, the only way you could let me down would be to tell me to leave, you know, walk out of here under some pretense of maintaining professional distance." She pointed toward the front of the house for emphasis. "I'm not sure how you feel about this, but I'm pretty sure that we can take on anything or anybody as long as we do it together. Right?" Jen watched a couple of tears slip down Terri's cheeks.

"Yes, Jen, absolutely yes." Terri lightly caressed her cheek with her thumb. "Together. Good."

Jen was back, fully in resolve mode. "Now, Ms. Big Bad Agent, how about if we eat this wonderful dinner that you worked so hard to make for me, and talk about something else."

Terri's expression softened. "Did you bring any movies?"

Happy to be back in her comfort zone, Jen smiled brightly and answered. "Yep, I brought both Tomb Raider films, *Aliens*, *Terminator 2*, *The Matrix*, *Underworld*, and *Resident Evil*." Grinning expectantly, she waited for a response.

Terri was finally laughing. "Jen, I'm sensing a theme here. Are you sure you didn't bring the last four seasons of *Voyager* with you too?"

Jen blushed. She was busted again. "Nope, I left those at home. Maybe next time."

CHAPTER SEVENTEEN

Saturday morning dawned clear and the day promised to be unseasonably warm. The local weatherman had forecast highs in the low seventies and abundant sunshine for the whole day. Terri could already see the strong sunlight filtering through the curtains of the bedroom. The air even smelled warm, but maybe that was because of last night. She smiled and stretched, shaking the cobwebs loose. Despite the late-night antics and subsequent pillow talk, she was up early. Her mind raced, as it frequently did, full of a mix of criminal facts and personal feelings that was responsible for waking her up. Despite the strong temptation, Terri hadn't brought up the case again after their initial dinner conversation. She opted instead to leave the heavy thinking to Jen, allowing her to voice her own fears and concerns when the time was right. And the time was definitely not right, not now.

Terri took a moment to study Jen's features as she slept in the bed next to her. Wild hair, peaceful expression, freckles across her nose, a little bit of a snore. Completely adorable. Despite the protestations of the night before, Terri wondered if either of them was prepared for the possibility of danger intruding on this perfect little space that was just the two of them. She also knew that if she spent too much time dwelling on the negative feelings that these thoughts were creating, she'd ruin the whole weekend, and their time together was short enough already.

Instead, she chose to let her thoughts trail back to the good stuff from the night before. Under the freckled nose and gee-whiz expression lurked the soul of a good old-fashioned horndog. Terri blushed as she remembered what had happened on the sofa in the media room as they attempted to watch a movie featuring yet another tank top–clad heroine, and then the attempted stargazing on the second-floor patio that left her with the belief that the neighbors would never be able to look her in the eye again. She continued to smile as she quietly rolled out of bed to use the bathroom.

Jen was stirring as Terri climbed back into bed. A sleepy voice asked, "What time is it?"

Terri leaned over to kiss the auburn hair, snuggling in at the same time. "It's early. Seven fifteen-ish. Go back to sleep."

Jen pulled her in closer, throwing an arm and a leg over her body. "I don't want to miss this time with you. Mmm, you're too soft and yummy."

Terri returned the snuggle, lightly stroking the bare leg and hip now firmly planted across her lower half. "So what did you have in mind for today?"

"Well, staying in bed all day would be my first plan, but I also have a Plan B that might interest you," Jen teased.

"Which is?"

"Which is this. You said last night that you missed the stars. Remember, on the patio?" Terri blushed again, recalling the events on the patio involving one chaise lounge and one college professor with an incredibly vivid imagination.

Jen grinned smugly. "From the color on your face, I see that you do remember. But the part I'm talking about is when you told me how much you miss seeing the stars in the city."

Terri thought for a second. "Go on."

"I know a place that's only a couple of hours from here where it's pitch black at night and you can see every star in the sky. And the hostess is incredibly accommodating to government agents. Especially gorgeous ones like you."

Terri thought a little more before adding, "And it is a long weekend…"

"Right, so I don't have to drive you back up here until Monday. Oh, there's also this nifty enchanted pond and a really cool little dog."

Terri had to laugh at these last two points. A spontaneous weekend in the country sounded great. It would also provide a great opportunity to see Jen in her own environment, which could go a long way toward easing the anxiety that seemed to color Terri's every thought. She finally answered, "Okay, I'm in. You want to leave soon?"

"How about showers and you load Jojo up with extra food, then we head out? We can get breakfast along the way."

"All right. But how about shower, singular?" She waggled her eyebrows and sat up to get out of bed, pulling Jen along behind her.

"Ooh, good plan, Agent McKinnon."

CHAPTER EIGHTEEN

Almost three hours later, after a stop for pancakes and to pick up Snickers, Jen pulled the 4Runner into the gravel drive of her farmhouse. She parked the car and released the little mutt with a command to "go do dog things." Snickers was off like a shot, flushing a rabbit out of the hedge that separated the front yard from the dirt road. Terri was tickled by the little beast's behavior. She was used to the reticence that cats possessed, but this dog was so much like its owner, and the word to describe Jen was anything but reticent. Tenacious, always moving, thinking, throwing herself into things with abandon, and always happy to be close to someone that she cared about, that was Jen. And Terri felt lucky to have found her. Jen spoke, breaking the reverie. "C'mon inside. We'll put your stuff up and then maybe I can show you my enchanted pond."

Terri grabbed her bags from the car and followed through the side door, the mudroom, and into the kitchen, the room she recognized from her first official trip. She'd been so focused on her previous visit that she had failed to notice the view of the Blue Ridge out the large bay window. They went through the living room to the small foyer and up the stairs. Jen was animated through the entire trip, pointing things out like the fireplace, the coat closet, the office, and the downstairs bathroom. Terri was looking at everything too, points of ingress and egress, traffic flow. At the top of the steps were the master bedroom and bathroom with adjoining dressing area and long walk-in closet. The guest room was across the hall. Terri was still counting windows and visually checking the type of locks on the doors. She was so lost in her own thoughts she didn't realize that Jen was speaking.

"Terri, did you hear me? Are you in there?" Jen waved a hand to call attention to herself standing next to the bed, in a kind of "hey, I'm over here" fashion.

Terri shook her head, lost in the acclimation process. She pushed the feeling aside and answered, "I'm sorry, I get this way. You know, new house, have to check it all out."

"I get it." Jen took her hands. "Sometimes you have to be Agent McKinnon first, right? I mean, that's okay. That's good." Terri smiled at the funny way that Jen put it, but noted that she was absolutely correct. "Besides, you know how I feel about Agent McKinnon." Jen was moving, closing the gap between them. "How she gets me all hot and bothered," pulling hands, moving closer, words breathed into an ear, "makes me want—"

Before she could finish the thought, Terri spun her around and backed her up against the wall. She hit with a dull thud, the impact forcing out a small grunt. Terri pinned Jen's hands to the wall and held her against the vertical surface, pressing forward with her entire body. Terri knew exactly what Jen wanted, knew that she wanted the same thing herself. To feel safe, to give her trust to someone, no matter what outrageous form that trust chose to embody.

Terri growled into Jen's ear, teasing out a whimper. "Is this what you want?" Jen nodded quickly in affirmation. Terri slid their hands up the wall, maintaining the contact until Jen's hands were over her head. She shifted to hold both hands using only one of hers, and now had a free hand available to check for concealed weapons. Running her fingers over Jen's cheek, Terri reached around to the back of her head and pulled their mouths together for a long, slightly rough kiss. Jen shook her head free to breathe as Terri fought to control the spinning in her own head. The intensity of the moment was threatening to overwhelm her, but the basic need to give everything she knew they both wanted drove her forward.

She slid her free hand down Jen's body, never losing contact, teasing around the small breasts through Jen's sweatshirt. Needing to be closer yet, Terri pulled up on the edge of the shirt, snaking her hand underneath. She pulled the tank top out of Jen's track pants with a quick yank to touch bare skin, her effort rewarded with a small moan as Jen mock-struggled, still pinned to the wall. Terri pressed forward with her body, using her hand to seek out and finally touch Jen's incredibly sensitive nipples, pinching first one then the other and back again, over and over, watching as Jen rolled her head against the wall, mouth open, eyes closed, breathing hard and fast.

Terri instinctively knew the situation called for immediate action, and eagerly complied. Sliding her hand down Jen's belly, she arrived at the top of the track pants and boxer shorts, and continued to push past the elastic waistbands of both articles, never breaking contact with skin or with the hands overhead still pinned to the wall. She felt soft curls and continued downward, seeking her goal as Jen continued to struggle, opening her legs a little wider and thrusting her hips toward the fingers that were now so close. Terri pushed her hand just a little farther, made contact with the copious wetness, and moaned "oh my God" as her own knees got slightly rubbery.

Clothes were decidedly in the way. Terri backed her hand

out enough to grab both waistbands and pulled them down, wrestling the garments off as Jen struggled to step out of them, still managing to maintain contact with her other hand overhead. Their combined actions managed to liberate one leg from the offending material, but that was enough for Terri to get her free hand quickly back to the earlier point of great interest. Stroking with her fingers just enough to get them lubricated, she pushed up and into Jen with two fingers, pulled out, added another, and thrust up again, harder and faster than the first time. Jen's response was more of a grunt than a moan, but it brought the weakness back to Terri's knees.

Finally releasing her grip overhead, Terri used her newly freed hand to grab Jen's ass, pulling her hips forward, supporting her weight as she continued the hard, deep thrusts. Since remaining upright was getting more and more difficult, Terri pulled Jen away from the wall, picking her up in the process, and dumped her rather unceremoniously on the bed. She held Jen to the mattress with her own body weight, straddling one leg, never once hesitating or slowing as Jen cried out and thrashed beneath her. Terri could feel Jen's leg grinding into her denim-clad crotch as Jen tensed. Since Jen's hands were over her head, much like they had been against the wall, Terri raised up enough to get on her knees and pin the hands back to the bed. That little reassertion of control was enough to send Jen over the edge, tensing and finally coming with a low, throaty growl of release. Terri still didn't stop, even as she felt the muscles contracting around her fingers. She kept right on thrusting, pushing Jen up and over a second time, and was soon rewarded with a second satisfied growl. This time, she did slow as Jen squeezed her thighs together, signaling that she could take no more.

"Terri, you have to stop." Jen panted out the words. "You're going to kill me here."

Terri released the hands that she still held firmly against the covers, and immediately arms wrapped around her back, pulling her into a needy, fierce hug. She gently pulled her fingers out, feeling the slender body that was holding her from below tense momentarily and then relax. Terri placed a series of little kisses along Jen's neck, noting the pulse beneath as it slowed to a more normal rhythm. The arms around her back finally loosened enough for her to sit up. She looked deeply into the eyes below her and watched with amazement and concern as a tear slipped out and rolled free.

"Jen, are you okay? Did I hurt you?" Terri was worried, but quickly relaxed once Jen reached up and squeezed her tightly again, letting her know that everything was indeed okay.

"No, no…I'm good." Jen let go of the hug to look back into Terri's eyes. "Perfect, even." Jen traced small lines with her fingers across Terri's forehead, down her temple, across her cheek. "I'm just a little overwhelmed by the way you make me feel. New stuff here, you know."

Terri sat back a little more. "New stuff?" She was surprised by the admission, not really knowing what Jen was trying to process, wondering if her actions had been too rough or demanding. "What kind of new stuff?"

Jen sat up, taking Terri's face in her hands. "I don't know if…I mean, I don't think I…you know, have the words." Terri watched, dumbstruck, as she realized that this adorable, wonderful person who normally had so much to say was now speechless.

"Take a breath, Jen. It'll come to you." She reached up to hold the hands that were still on her face, pulling them down but never releasing them. "You can tell me anything, you know?"

A smile started at the corners of Jen's mouth while she took one more calming breath and finally relaxed enough to talk again. "Okay, here goes…Terri McKinnon, you are, without doubt, the most amazing and wonderful person that I have ever met." Another deep breath. "And I feel like I want to spend forever showing you how amazing and wonderful you are. Do you get it?"

"Yeah, I do get it." Terri released the hands that she was still holding, touching the freckled face, pulling Jen in for a soft, gentle kiss. "I really do get it."

"So, what do you think?"

The wide-eyed innocence was back, stealing Terri's breath away as she tried to speak, knowing that there was only one answer to that question. "I think I love you too."

Terri watched, fascinated, as Jen's eyes, wet with unshed tears, bored into her own. Nothing else mattered. The distance between them diminished until lips touched softly, granting the contact they both desperately wanted. Jen's lips parted, moving slowly, and a tentative tongue slipped past to touch her own. They both shuddered at the intimacy.

Time slowed to a crawl as Terri leaned back against the comforter, barely aware of the hands on her shoulders lightly pushing her down. The kiss never slowed, even as she felt her motion halted by the mattress beneath her, the warm weight of Jen's body holding her in place. Terri allowed her hands to wander up and under the ribbed fabric of a tank top, back down to the small of Jen's back, and up again, pulling both undershirt and sweatshirt off on the way up.

Jen backed out of the kiss long enough to get the clothing over her head, and finally broke the silence. "You have way too many clothes on." Terri watched again as Jen's small hands disappeared under the navy blue of her FBI sweatshirt, pushing toward her breasts, stopping as the hands found what they were looking for. It was difficult to tell who moaned louder as Terri felt her breasts being massaged through the satiny spandex of her sports bra. She knew Jen could feel it too as her nipples hardened to the touch and her back arched. Jen backed her hands out enough to get under the bra, pushing it and the sweatshirt off over Terri's head.

Terri had to smile as her lack of clothing seemed to mesmerize Jen, who could do nothing but stare and lick her lips. "Jen?"

Jen shook her head, breaking her own reverie. "Sorry, I'll just never get used to how glorious your…"

Terri silenced the statement with a fingertip to Jen's lips, and two simple words: "Show me."

So she did. Lowering her head, Jen kissed Terri's right breast, taking a circuitous route around the nipple as she used her hand to lightly knead at the left one. Terri twined her fingers into Jen's hair and applied just enough pressure to make her intentions clear. Jen responded, swirling her tongue around the nipple that she'd been avoiding, and finally bit down gently, sending out a familiar jolt of electricity that made Terri hiss and arch her back, seeking a firmer touch wherever she could find it. Jen continued, teasing as she backed away, and turned her attention to the other nipple. She repeated the swirl/bite tactic, garnering the same response as Terri squirmed under the attention and pulled harder on the back of Jen's head. Terri felt Jen's body, still holding her to the bed, raise up enough to shift and straddle her leg, applying pressure with a naked thigh against the crotch of her blue jeans.

Jen groaned and teased just a little more. "Agent McKinnon, I hate to tell you this, but your jeans are kind of wet. Maybe you should take them off."

Terri teased right back. "Well, Dr. Rosenberg, since it's your fault that they're wet, maybe you should take them off."

Jen eagerly complied, sitting up to undo the buttons of the offending garment. Standing, she pulled off Terri's sneakers and grabbed both hems of the pants, pulling hard enough to remove them in one relatively smooth motion, then returned to remove Terri's underwear. She grabbed one foot on its return trip to the bed and kissed a wet trail, starting at Terri's ankle, up past her knee, all the way to the top of her inner thigh, where she paused just long enough to arrange herself back on the bed, make eye contact, and waggle her eyebrows. Terri returned the waggle with a sultry glance and a nod as she began to chew lightly on her lower lip, giving silent encouragement for Jen to continue her trip northward. Jen did exactly that, rubbing her face in the soft, dark brown curls, nestling between the lips into the warm wetness, and gently extended her tongue to collect a taste. Terri again pushed on the back of Jen's head, telling her what she needed, encouraging her to keep going. Jen complied, using her mouth and tongue to nibble and lick, ever upward until she found Terri's swollen clit. She pulled it into her mouth and sucked hard, drawing out a long moan as Terri pushed even harder on the back of her head, wordlessly begging for more.

Terri was vaguely aware that the rest of the world, as well as her powers of speech, were quickly slipping away, replaced by the pinpoint focus of Jen's mouth on her clit as she continued to suck, flicking lightly from side to side with her tongue. Terri released her death grip on Jen's head, reaching up to grab the rails of the headboard with both hands, and thrust her hips up to solidify the contact. Moaning again, she became aware of slender fingers playing around her opening, so she pushed down with her hips in an attempt to telegraph her need. Jen teased, staying close with her fingers, but not giving Terri what she so desperately wanted. Terri kept trying, actually begging, "Jen, please..."

But still no fingers. She felt the first spark of her orgasm as she continued to reach for the elusive touch, dancing maddeningly away the more she tried to capture it. Desperation forced her to beg again, panting, "Jen, fuck me, please...I need—"

Terri never finished her request as Jen finally gave in, entering her hard with two fingers, commencing a rhythm that soon had Terri screaming out, invoking deities, and swearing like a truck driver. She came hard, harder than she'd ever come before for anyone, a combination of release and relief from having been teased so mercilessly. Slowly returning to planet Earth, relaxing from the intense sensation, she regained her focus and looked down to see a beautiful freckled face, complete with a wicked little grin that reminded Terri of exactly why she'd finally let go and fallen in love.

"Jen, that was evil."

Jen waggled her eyebrows again and continued to smile. "Does that mean you didn't like it?"

"No. I didn't say that. It's just not nice to tease a woman who carries a gun."

Jen laughed hard and crawled up Terri's body to give her a kiss. "You don't scare me. You're a marshmallow and I'm the only one who knows it. Makes me kind of special, don't you think?"

Terri looked into Jen's eyes, her mood getting a little more serious. "You're the most special thing that's ever happened to me." Terri pulled her closer for a snuggle, unable to brush aside a momentary unease about their future. "Don't ever forget that."

CHAPTER NINETEEN

Terri watched Jen pick up the neon pink tennis ball and give it a long toss down the hill. Snickers sped off after it, tail raised high like the flag on a dune buggy, making him easy to follow as he bounded through the tall weeds. The day was still warm and bathed in a soft light that promised a glorious sunset in less than an hour.

After spending a large portion of the afternoon being physically shown how amazing and wonderful she was, Terri was happy. Happy with a great big ol' side order of smitten. She'd been content with her life before, but couldn't imagine ever going back to that now that she had this new thing, this exceptional feeling of ease and excitement. She was vaguely aware that everything, every sight, smell, and sound, seemed both heightened and softened at the same time. And she became aware, beyond any shadow of a doubt, that she would do anything to protect the source of that new light in her life.

Terri watched with more than a little amusement as Jen cursed at Snickers for ignoring the ball once again to take off after some four-legged critter that proved to be much more animated than the game his mom was offering. Her attention was drawn to the backside of that person, bent over, pawing through weeds, looking for a pink tennis ball. Smitten, yes, that was the right word. So engrossed was she in the view that she failed to notice when Jen looked up from knee level and busted her, mid-leer.

"See something you like, Agent McKinnon?"

Terri flushed at the question, knowing she'd been caught. Definitely enjoying the view, but there was so much more to it. Words were not available, not at that precise moment, so she just nodded and kept moving forward to catch up. As Terri closed the gap, Jen held out her hand, grabbed Terri's, and pulled her in for a quick hug and a kiss. Leaning back but not letting go, Jen asked, "Terri, are you okay? You're awfully quiet."

Terri backed out of the embrace, pulled a weed from the ground, and wrapped it around her finger, idly fiddling with it to help her thought process. "I'm okay. To quote someone near and dear, perfect even." She pulled the weed out straight and began to wind it around her finger in the opposite direction. "Also a little overwhelmed. You know, this is new for me too." She resumed walking down the hill toward the pond, and Jen quickened her pace to catch up. "I've always known exactly where I should be and what I should be doing, and now all I want to think about is how I can stay right here and never let you out of my sight." Jen started to interject, but Terri stopped her with a raised palm. "I know what you're going to say, and I know that you can take care of yourself, but don't you see? I want to do it. I want to take care of you, and feed you, and keep you warm at night, and love you all the time. And as much as you don't want to talk about this, there's at least half a chance there's someone out there who might want to hurt you. I just can't have that, but I'm also not sure what I can do to stop it." She let the weed flutter to the ground. "Hence the introspective silence."

Jen took Terri by the arm and pulled her to the right, down the path to the pond. Terri watched as her comments sank in and Jen thought for a moment before speaking. "Terri, listen. I know what you mean. I feel kind of exposed myself right now. I don't want to talk about whatever it is that's going on, but not because I don't think about it." She found Snickers's ball along the path and gave it a toss. He followed this time and found it. "I don't talk about it because I know there's really nothing I can do. And I'm fully aware that there's not much you can do about it either. I didn't say what I said to you earlier out of some need to be protected. I said it because I love you and I care about you, and a very large part of me wants to protect and take care of you. I think that's a big part of what love really is."

Jen hesitated as Snickers returned with the ball. After taking it from him, she held it out to Terri, offering her the chance to play with the little mutt. Terri took the ball and threw a perfect strike, cringing as it landed with an audible splash in the pond. Snickers ran after it, but applied the brakes before he hit the water.

Jen looked at Terri with a bit of awe. "Nice toss."

Terri blushed. "Thank you." She felt the familiar pull as Jen slid in close to her. "I suppose now you're going to tell me that ball players make you hot too."

"Would it make me shallow if I said yes?" Jen helped herself to a couple of playful nips along Terri's neck.

Terri's head was spinning with the attention and the heat of the moment. "Would it make me shallow if I told you that I have a weak spot for adorable college professors?"

Jen rubbed her chin and thought with mock seriousness. "Hmm, I don't know. I think I need more details before I answer that."

God, she was cute. "How about adorable college professors who, no matter how hard they try not to, seem to wind up involved with the FBI?"

Jen laughed and stood back, taking the agent by the hands. "That, Agent McKinnon, would make you a raving genius. Definitely not shallow."

"Good. Then I guess we're both exactly where we need to be." Terri leaned in to collect a sloppy, wet kiss from the painfully cute object of her desire. "Well, exactly where we need to be, minus the chill and impending darkness." She took Jen by the hand, pulling her along the path back to the house. "I need something warm to drink and a cuddle."

Jen happily came along, whistling for Snickers to follow. He ran alongside, bounding and hoping for a ball to chase. Jen apologized to him. "Sorry, little dude. Take it up with her." She jerked a thumb toward Terri. "She's the one that pulled the Roger Clemens and lost your ball."

"Hey, that's not fair." Terri let go of Jen's hand and gave her a playful little shove. "I'll get him a new one."

"Darn tootin' you will."

CHAPTER TWENTY

Just a quick trip to the office supply store and the drugstore. No big deal. Just pick up a couple of things.

Bradley Allen Davis had told his boss that he needed to go down to the south end of town to do a little shopping. Grooming supplies. Who would question that? Everyone needs stuff for their hair. Business-sized envelopes? Hey, time to file your taxes. Everyone else was doing that. One illegal cell phone and an automatic weapon. Slightly more difficult to explain, but not hard to come by if you knew the right people.

He knew the right people. He also knew the right way to start a fire, both literally and metaphorically. The right kind of hair product, some chemicals borrowed from the public pool across the street, and a couple of medium business-sized envelopes would light up someone's house just fine, and, if he was lucky, burn it to the ground. That was the literal fire.

The metaphorical fire was even better. It was time to let everyone know what they needed to know to get things burning even hotter. That's where the illegal cell phone came in. A couple of well-placed calls would set the ball rolling toward the conclusion of his plan. They all needed to know that he was on his way. And now they would all know just where he was going.

He walked into Staples, found the envelopes, paid cash, and was out the door in less than ten minutes. Then the easy trip across Stadium Boulevard to Arbor Drugs, emerging less than fifteen minutes later with a large tube of Brylcreem (a little dab'll do ya) and a carton of cigarettes. Back in the car for the haul down Stadium Boulevard to the not-so-nice part of Ypsilanti, a great place to pick up a cell phone and a little more recreational headache medicine. Back home again in less than two hours. All in all, a pretty successful trip.

The pool chemicals were easy enough. Just wait until after dark when the junior ice hockey leagues started at the facility across the street. Walk around the side to the large garage door where the Zamboni was parked and simply open the door to the pool chemical storage area. One plastic cup and one large Ziploc bag, and he now had everything he needed to light things up once and for all. He tossed the cup in the trash can next to the skate park. Fingerprints or no, he was never coming back here.

He was back safe and sound in his apartment by eight o'clock. He started a new pot of coffee and lit another cigarette on the burner of the stove. Booting up the laptop, which was the only computer left of his collection, he started to look for a back way into the files of the Federal Bureau of Investigation. It would certainly take some time, but any door could be opened, if you had the right key. He was pretty sure that individual case information wasn't available, but he didn't really need that. Just the database of agents and the number to the central switchboard.

The cell phone numbers had been a little difficult to get, but again, he had the right key. The numbers he needed were now safely stored in the memory of the phone, ready to go when he was. Speed dial number one called the FBI.

"Good evening, Federal Bureau of Investigation. How may I direct your call?"

"I might have some information about a case and I need to talk to the agent in charge."

"Let me put you through to investigations. Please hold."

Bradley waited as the hold music came on. Even the FBI had hold music. What is this world coming to? At least it wasn't John Tesh. That would have been more than his migraine could stand. He waited for less than a minute for a human to answer the phone.

"Agent Stansfield."

"Good evening, Agent Stansfield. I have a pressing need to speak to the agent in charge of the NoVaGenEx case. Is that person available?" Bradley lit another cigarette, mindful of the fact that this call needed to be as short as possible.

"Sir, that would be Agent McKinnon, and she's not in the office now. Perhaps I could—"

"No, thank you. I'll call back." With that, he hit the button on the phone to terminate the call. Less than a minute thirty. Not too bad considering that he'd been on hold for most of that. He turned his attention back to the screen of the laptop that now displayed the agent database. "Agent McKinnon, wonder what you look…whoa…nice lookin'. Hello, sweetie. We're going to have some really interesting things to talk about, I think." He cut and pasted the identification photo onto the desktop of the computer, adding it to the file simply marked "photos."

Bradley lit another Marlboro, inhaled deeply, and returned to the screen of the laptop. Next stop, James Madison University mail server, looking for a back door, once again proving that he had the key. He looked over the lines of code that jumped

to life on the screen, tilting his head to redirect the smoke that
curled upward from the glowing end of the cigarette. He knew
where to find who he was looking for. Now he just had to find
one friend to send her a little message.

He started stabbing at random lines of code, looking for
the one that would lead him to the common thread. "There
she is…let's see who you've been e-mailing." He hummed a
little as he looked through the hacked mailbox. Personal mail
would be better, but work mail was faster, easier to get into.
"Aha!" He found the inbox, looking through the headers for
anything personal. "What's this?" He opened the mail from
one McKinnon, T., from a server in Northern Virginia . "Well,
well, Dr. Rosenberg. You've got a new girlfriend, and she's the
agent in charge of your case. How about that?" Bradley almost
rubbed his hands together in glee.

He followed the e-mail trail back to Agent McKinnon and
started reading. "Fuel for the fire. I love it."

❖

Jen was awake despite the darkness outside and the large
green numbers on the clock that displayed 4:17. She was
awake because the phone rang not once, but twice before she
could dig it out of her briefcase.

"What the fuck?" Jen was confused. Since she had been
asleep, she didn't realize right away that the call that woke her
up was actually a text message. A very cryptic text message.
"Thirty-six, eighty-nine, what? Forty-three." Something
clicked. Something in the back of her thoughts, an old memory.
"Seventeen." She knew that was the next number. Even before
she saw it, she knew that seventeen was the next number. "Oh,
shit."

Brad. She knew it was Brad. These numbers were the

password for the job they had been working on. The one that landed Brad in prison. They were burned into her memory from ten years ago, but they stood out like neon lights in the window of a bar. Jen was terrified.

She hit the speed dial number one to call Terri, forgetting that it was way before five a.m. The sleepy voice that answered soothed her frazzled nerves a little.

"Jen, sweetie, what time is it?"

Jen pulled the phone away to look at the time and winced. "Um, it's four twenty. Sorry to wake you." She felt instantly bad for blowing Terri out of bed this early, but it couldn't be avoided. "I need your help." Before Terri could even get an answering question out, Jen launched into an explanation. "It's him, Terri. I know it's him."

"Who? Jen, what are you talking about?"

"Brad. It's him. I don't care what the parole guy in Ann Arbor keeps telling you, this is Brad. He's killing people and it's all for my benefit."

She was almost hysterical, but Terri's little shushing noises and calm voice brought her back to Earth. "It can't be. He's being supervised."

"I don't care." Jen was back to hysterical. "It's him. I can prove it."

Terri sounded a little more awake. "Sweetie, calm down. Tell me what happened."

Jen took a long breath to calm herself down. "Okay, I was asleep. Well, no duh, it's four twenty in the morning. Anyway, my phone buzzed. I thought it was a call at first, but it turned out to be a text message. A string of numbers. I didn't recognize them at first, but now I know."

"What were the numbers?"

Jen didn't even have to look at her phone to recall the string of digits. "Thirty-six, eighty-nine—"

Terri provided the next one. "Forty-three."

"Yes, and seventeen. Terri, how do you know about this?"

Terri sighed and tried to explain. "We've seen these numbers. A little artistic touch left by the gunman."

"Artistic touch? What the fuck are you talking about?" Jen was getting really agitated again. She paced the floor in the kitchen like a tiger in a cage. "And if you knew about this, why didn't you tell me?"

"Sweetie, calm down. Let's just say that we found these numbers at each crime scene. We had no idea what they meant, so we kept it out of the public information. I couldn't tell you."

"Oh, jeez, Terri. That's crazy. You could have told me this right away and you and Bobby wouldn't have been banging your heads against the wall for all this time."

"Jen, I'm sorry. It's my job and that's what the Bureau decided was appropriate." Jen was starting to calm down a little. "Since we didn't know what the numbers meant, we had to keep them confidential just so no one decided to copycat anything. It would have screwed up the sequence, and we needed it intact to learn what it meant. I've got half the cryptologists in the Bureau working on this." Terri sounded apologetic. "I didn't want to keep things from you, but it looked like Brad was in the clear, so we didn't pursue him."

"Great. Just fucking great." Jen slid down the front of her kitchen cabinet to sit on the floor. "There's only one number left. I'm sorry, Terri, I know this isn't your fault, but—"

"But my hands were tied. Jen, I can fix this. I'm up now. I'll call Bobby and have him come get me and we'll head to the office right now to see what we can find out from the police in Ann Arbor. Will you be all right until then?"

Jen stayed tucked in her ball on the floor, as she sniffed and wiped her nose with a dishtowel. "I don't have much choice, do I?" Snickers was up and out of bed, waiting patiently to see what was going on.

Terri's calm voice answered, "No, I guess you don't. Keep the phone close in case you need to call for help. Just hold tight and I'll be in touch as soon as I can, even if I don't know what's going on. But I will find out, I promise you."

"I know you will. Call me soon, okay?" Jen didn't want the phone call to end, because then she really would be alone. "And don't forget that I love you."

"I know you do...I love you too. Now sit tight for a couple of hours and I'll call you back. I have to go catch a bad guy."

Jen finally relented. "Okay, bye." She closed the phone so Terri could go to work. She laughed weakly and directed her next comment to Snickers. "And now the ritual hiding begins."

CHAPTER TWENTY-ONE

The ride to the office was almost silent. When Bobby had arrived to pick her up at the ungodly early hour, Terri had been agitated. She had bounded out the door as soon as he arrived, nearly knocking him back down her front steps. She had gone over Jen's phone call again in a rush and answered all of Bobby's questions before they climbed into the car. Now she sat, staring out the window of Bobby's car into the darkness at nothing, but her mind was still racing. She ticked off the mental checklist of everything she had already done since Jen's phone call. First was the call to Bobby, who may or may not have been alone when she called but dropped everything for her as he always did. She had already called the office to have them contact the Ann Arbor Police Department and pick this Davis guy up, but she had one more call to make—this one to Davis's parole officer to find out if he knew about his parolee's activities or if he simply had his head up his ass. Bobby just drove, giving her the time she needed to process and make sense of what needed to be done.

As they pulled into a parking space, she had the door to the car open before he could slip the car into park. She was on a mission as she strode purposefully toward the building entrance. Bobby sprinted to catch up to her. "Terri, slow down."

She kept right on walking. "You know as well as I do that we need to work fast here." He caught her arm, so she stopped to breathe. "Bobby, we don't know where he was calling from. For all I know, he's in Harrisonburg by now. Jen said there was only one number left." She shuddered at the thought. "We can slow down when I know where the phone call came from, okay?" Without waiting for his response, she took off again, determined to find answers as quickly as possible.

Terri swiped her ID through the magnetic card reader at the entrance. She pushed the door hard enough for it to stay open for Bobby, but never slowed as she flashed her ID to the agent at the desk and strode toward the elevators. She pushed the button, but nothing happened. She punched it again, actually several more times, but still no elevator. "God dammit." She turned hard to the left to use the stairs.

The office was mostly empty, save for the two agents on staff for the night shift. They jumped as Terri stormed into the space and started barking orders, getting everyone on the phone with somebody. Stansfield jumped on the phone and called to get the status from the Ann Arbor police. They had already been told to dispatch a team of officers, armed and ready for resistance, to the apartment of Bradley Allen Davis. Stansfield had even gone as far as to suggest they send a SWAT team.

Terri tossed the folder of information about the parole officer onto Bobby's desk, pointing at it for emphasis. "Please call this asshole and find out—" She stopped to breathe when she saw the wide-eyed expression on his face. "Sorry, Bobby. I'm a little tense here." One more calming breath. "Will you please call this…gentleman…and find out what is going on with Davis? I'd hate to rip his head off over the phone. Especially at six a.m."

Bobby took the folder with a quiet "Sure, Terri. No problem."

The calm was temporary. Terri pointed to the last agent in the room, a new guy that she didn't recognize. "Hey, newbie. Is there any coffee?" The poor guy jumped and squeaked out a yes. "Please, will you get some for all of us? Thank you." She was now satisfied that everyone was in place doing the right thing. Seemed like a good time to call and check on Jen. Before Terri could get her cell phone out of her pocket, the phone on her desk rang sharply. She practically dove on it, picked up the handset, and answered in her best composed-agent voice. "Agent McKinnon."

The man's voice on the other end was calm. "Agent Terri McKinnon? I believe you and I have some things to talk about."

"We do?"

Terri heard the sharp inhalation on the other end. Cigarette, she recognized immediately.

He continued, "Yes, Agent McKinnon, we do. Some of your friends came to call, but I really wasn't prepared for company. I'd rather have a little chat with you. How about that?"

She slid into her chair, perching on the edge, and thought for just a second before answering, "That sounds like a good idea. Mr. Davis, I presume." She stayed as calm as possible but began gesturing wildly to get Bobby's attention. Taking the largest red marker from the pencil cup on the desk, she slid her legal pad in front of her and scribbled TRACE THIS big enough so Bobby could see it without having to ask why. He looked up to see her pointing at the phone, so he ended his call to the parole officer without saying good-bye and dialed the switchboard to put a trace on the line. He gave her a thumbs-up that she returned as an okay sign, and she turned her attention back to the call. Davis was waiting patiently.

"Agent McKinnon...Terri. May I call you Terri?"

"No, Mr. Davis, you may not. Why did you call me?" Terri's heart pounded and her hand gripped the phone tightly.

Cigarette again. "Well, then, Agent McKinnon, we'll do this your way. I can only assume that you've got a trace on this line, but I'd like to assure you that this phone will be on the bottom of the Huron River before the trace finds it. But please, feel free to try." He chuckled, obviously amused at his own ingenuity. "That is your job, after all."

Terri's exasperation threatened to come through, but she maintained her calm demeanor and measured, clipped tones. "Yes, Mr. Davis, that is my job. But you still haven't answered my question. Why do you think we need to talk?"

She heard the lighter this time, a Zippo, as he lit another cigarette.

"Well, I think that you and I just might have a mutual friend." She cringed, waiting for the blow to land. "A cute little college professor named Jennifer Rosenberg. Have you met her yet?"

Terri tried the dodge as she wrestled with her own panic. "Why would you think I know this person?"

Inhalation again. "Because you are the agent in charge of the NoVaGenEx case, and I'd be willing to bet that you interviewed at least one person from the company. And since she's close to you, geographically speaking of course, and she happened to attend college in my neck of the woods, I figured that you two might have met."

Terri continued the evasion. "Well, I'd have to check my notes, but—"

"Oh, please, Agent McKinnon, let's not do this. I know you've talked with her. I know you've had dinner with her." Terri knew right then and there that he had her. It only got worse when he started quoting from Terri's own e-mail. "I miss watching you sleep, and wonder what you dream about. You've brought light back into my life."

Shit. He really had her. He knew, but she had to keep it together. "Regardless of what you think you know, what does this have to do with what you wanted from me?" She looked across to Bobby and shrugged, silently asking for the status of the trace on the phone. He shook his head and motioned with his hand for her to keep him talking.

"I'm sure she told you all about me and my little, shall we say, side trip to Terre Haute. Right?" He waited long enough for dramatic pause, but not long enough for her to answer. "Never mind, I'm sure she did. I just wanted to return the favor. Maybe tell you a thing or two about our friend Dr. Rosenberg."

Terri continued to wait in silence. She figured that this was his show and he'd keep talking no matter what she said. He continued, drawing on the third cigarette of the conversation. "Did she hit on you first, Agent McKinnon? Show up to take you to lunch?" Terri gasped, unable to control the knee-jerk reaction.

Davis chuckled. "Hmm, I guess by that reaction that she did. She does that, you know? Likes to hit on pretty girls, and you most certainly fall into that category."

Terri was dumbstruck, but pressed on. "Mr. Davis, again I see nothing here that we need to discuss. So if you—"

His tone changed, became sharper, more aggressive. "She likes to stick her nose in where it doesn't belong too. I taught her how to hack into banks, you know. Is she still playing with that little hobby? Or did you people figure out how to make it all go away again?"

Terri was now fully enraged, but she resisted the urge to come to Jen's defense. She wouldn't give Davis the satisfaction.

He continued, a bit more settled this time, "Again, I just want to make sure you're looking into all of the guilty parties here with your investigation. Leaving no stone unturned, as it were. Sometimes things are not always what they seem to be."

Terri noticed Bobby waving, indicating that they had the trace. He quickly scribbled MICHIGAN on the notepad, allowing her at least a second to relax.

Not long, however, as Davis continued his rant. "Sorry to cut this short, but it has been a pleasure, Agent McKinnon. We'll talk again soon. Please send my regards to Jennifer, okay? Thank you so much for your time, but I really need to say good-bye now. Have a wonderful day." With that, the call was terminated.

Terri hung up the phone and slumped forward in her chair, resting her head on the desk. She looked at Bobby to answer the concerned look on his face. "God, what an arrogant prick." She turned enough to see the newbie agent standing next to her desk, holding a steaming Styrofoam cup of coffee in one shaking hand. Accepting the hot drink, she smiled her best smile and simply said thank you. It wasn't even six fifteen and she was already worn out.

"Bobby, where's the Advil?"

Bradley sat in the rental car with his knit cap pulled low and a heavy scarf over his face, looking to all the world like a typical late February commuter in Michigan. After sitting patiently as what looked like most of the Ann Arbor Police Department screamed into the parking lot across the street, he made his phone call, fucked with the FBI, and watched most of the police, as well as the big guns of the SWAT team, leave the parking lot. Laughing, he shook his head, tossed the phone out the window into the trash can, and pulled out onto Jackson Avenue. Two green lights later and he was on I-94 leaving Ann Arbor. He hoped it was forever.

❖

Terri was finally able to relax a little. She had even managed a quiet apology to the newbie guy for demanding coffee. Things were working now. The police were there. She held no illusions that they would capture Davis. She knew full well that he was one step ahead of them. But he was still in Michigan, and that bought her several hours. There was still much to think about, but she put most of it aside long enough to call Jen. She must have been sitting with the phone in her hand. It only rang once before she answered.

"Terri, oh thank God. What's going on?"

Terri left her desk and walked across the hallway and into the ladies' room to find some privacy. Using her soft girlfriend voice, which was even calmer than her soft agent voice, she explained the entire situation. That the police were there now, that the parole officer was shocked at the events, and that she'd actually spoken with Davis. She heard a chuckle from the other end of the call.

"How many cigarettes did he smoke?"

Terri laughed, slightly amazed that Jen could find humor even in the middle of this mess. "I counted three and we were on the phone for less than ten minutes. Maybe he'll die of lung cancer before he can—" She stopped, fearful of letting too much information pass to Jen that would frighten her further.

"Before he can what?"

She took a breath. "Jen, as soon as you called earlier, I called the office to get the Ann Arbor police to go pick him up, but he was waiting. He anticipated our move. I haven't seen a report yet, but he couldn't have called me if the police found him first. We do know that he is still in Michigan, so we still have a little time."

Terri heard the slight tremble in her voice as Jen asked, "Not much time, though, right?"

"No, but we have people at the local airports with his photo and description. That leaves ground transportation as his only option, and that gives us at least twelve hours to work with, hopefully more." She hoped that her tone was controlled enough to cover her anxiety about what they still didn't know.

"Uh-huh. And then what?"

God, she was really starting to feel stupid as well as unarmed. "And then we talk to the police and see if they found anything in his apartment." This was not the comfort she'd hoped to provide. "Based on that, Bobby and I draw up a plan for the boss, and maybe head down to your place."

Terri could hear Jen relax a little more after learning that she might have personal support. "You going to be the cavalry, Agent McKinnon? Come riding in here in your big black truck and save my skinny ass?" She paused for a second. "I like that idea. Well, certainly better than the one where a psycho whackjob comes riding in here in his Rent-a-Wreck and blows my brains out. I'll definitely take what's behind door number one, thank you."

Terri cringed as the "blows my brains out" idea struck home. She was also hearing enough of Jen's patented false bravado to know that she was terrified. "Jen, I think you should probably try to go to school today. Do what you normally do. Stay in public places with people nearby. Keep the phone close and I'll call as soon as I know anything else." She hoped that would be enough. Lowering her voice, she hoped that she had enough confidence left to pull off one last comment. "I won't let him hurt you. You know that, right?"

"Yeah, Terri, I know that. You know that I love you, right?"

"Yeah, Jen, I know that too. Try to relax, have a normal day, and I'll call you soon."

Jen sounded small as she said, simply, "Okay, bye."

Terri snapped the phone closed and returned to the office. Damn, this was hard.

The tension was palpable. Everyone in the office was sitting on the edge of a knife blade, unable to do anything but wait and watch her, evidently. The loss of objectivity was the worst part. Terri had never faced anything quite like this before. She was scared, and that was never good when the one thing she needed most of all was a clear, level head. All of the bullshit that Davis had thrown her way about Jen's past was floating around in her head, intermingled with the tension. It really sucked that he knew about her relationship with Jen. It was almost like he had been counting on it, but there was no way for him to know that it would happen. Was there? She was sure it had all been carefully calculated to throw the investigation off track. She dismissed it as the rantings of a lunatic who was trying to keep her off balance. That's why he had called, just to fuck with her. And it had worked.

She stopped behind Bobby on the way back to her own desk, put a hand on his shoulder, and asked, "Anything yet?"

"We don't have much. Davis was gone, just like you thought, and his apartment was cleaned out. Ann Arbor already issued the APB. The cell phone was in a trash can across the street. The only thing they found was four overflowing ashtrays and a note. They're faxing us a copy of it. I'll just go check and see if it's here."

Since there was nothing to do but wait until the fax arrived,

Terri availed herself of the time to pull out the rest of the case files from the drawer. The largest file had all the information regarding the first four attacks. She shook her head. They could have spent the next six months looking for patterns that didn't exist in the numbers found at the crime scenes. "Shit," she muttered under her breath. If she had been able to tell Jen about the numbers, this would have all been over and done with already, but now Davis had managed to elude them. Also, the fact that there were additional attacks at all seemed simply bizarre. If he wanted Jen, why didn't he just go get her? It was becoming all too apparent that Bradley Allen Davis was playing with them, and perhaps working up to a big finish. Why was pretty obvious. He was nuts, driven by a need for revenge for his prison abuse and subsequent health problems. What Terri didn't know was when. Would he go directly to Virginia, or was there somewhere else he needed to stop first? More questions, no answers.

She was just about to slam her hands onto the desk in frustration when Bobby reappeared with the fax. He said nothing, but he looked worried. He handed the papers to Terri. It was the preliminary police report, just a brief summary of information that they already knew. The apartment was empty, the computer was gone, and everything else was gone with the exception of the original of the second fax—one single page that knocked the breath from her and would have dropped her to her knees if she'd been standing. A computer-generated image, blown up to eight by ten, of the Virginia driver's license photo of one Dr. Jennifer Rosenberg. The complete series of numbers, just as Jen had described, was scrawled across her face in bold marker strokes, with one simple message to be delivered.

Tell Jen I'll see her in Hell.

CHAPTER TWENTY-TWO

He drove east into the sunrise for a short while, then headed south on I-75 into Ohio and toward his next destination. The rental car, while adequate, provided little comfort for his throbbing head, so he took a small one-hit pipe from his shirt pocket, sparked the Zippo to life, and applied flame to the small bud in the bowl. Inhaling deeply, he felt the first warm glow of relief as the unfiltered smoke tore into his ragged throat. "Not too much. No need to get pulled over." Not when he was getting so close to the completion of his plan. One more little detail to take care of, then he was taking a side trip to the Commonwealth of Kentucky.

This part of the plan was the most complicated, but would throw the biggest monkey wrench into the investigation. He took one more hit off the weed before returning the bowl to his shirt pocket. He had everything he needed for the next step, with one exception. A decoy. Someone who looked enough like him to waylay the FBI for twenty-four hours. The decoy would be a tricky find, but Bradley Allen Davis was in control now, and since he was now officially calling the shots, he could take a little time to find what he needed. And it was a long way from Michigan to Kentucky, so time was his ally.

The phone call to the FBI had been a lot of fun. Those

people were always so cool. Agent McKinnon was definitely not one to be trifled with, but he sensed a weakness. Actually, he had heard that weakness. One small shift in her demeanor when he'd asked about Rosenberg. That meant he had her. It also meant that he'd need to be careful how he handled her from here on out. Since Rosenberg had managed to weasel her way into the good graces of the FBI by working the romantic angle with Agent McKinnon, things might get tricky. But he still had plenty of time to worry about that. It was time to start checking out the rest stops and roadside spots for the right hitchhiker.

❖

Terri was still doing her best caged animal impersonation when McNally finally arrived in the office a little before eight a.m. He had some knowledge about the situation but needed to be brought up to speed. Motioning for Bobby and Terri, he strode into his own office, sat at his desk, folded his hands on the flat surface, and asked, "What's going on?"

Terri immediately launched into the full rundown, including the text message that Jen had received, Terri's phone call from Davis, and the police report from Ann Arbor. She left out the part where Davis knew that she and Jen had been seeing each other. She was doing her best to control her own raging anxiety, but McNally hadn't spent thirty years at the Bureau without learning a thing or two about human behavior. She knew that he would certainly sense something from her that he'd never seen before, and that could make things complicated.

He looked right at Terri, staring holes into her, and asked again. "What's going on?"

She quickly decided that the best course of action was innocence, however feigned. "Sir?"

"McKinnon, I've watched you for the last seven years. You are one cool cookie…usually. Is there something about this Rosenberg person that I should know about? Something, shall we say, outside of the case?"

Terri felt the rage begin to bubble through, pushing aside the anxiety. Fortunately for her, rage was easier controlled than anxiety. "Sir, I don't know what you could possibly be suggesting, but we have a potential death threat here, made against an innocent citizen, and I…we have the power to stop it. I don't understand why we're still sitting here."

"I suppose you're right. So what's your plan?"

Terri felt herself shift into efficient agent mode as she explained the plan. "Agent Kraft and I will go down to Mount Crawford. Since we know that ground transportation is Davis's only option, we figured we have at least twelve hours to work. Minus, of course, the two hours for the trip." McNally nodded his consent, indicating that she should continue. "We call the county sheriff and request some vehicular support, check the perimeter of the property, and secure the house."

"And then what? Do you want to consider moving her somewhere?"

Terri jumped on the answer before he could even finish the question. "No, sir. I really don't think that's necessary. Her house is far more secure than any hotel, and Davis has proven to be adept at locating her as well as her acquaintances. The home has limited entrances, there's no risk of civilian interference, and she's more familiar with the surroundings."

"She knows the best places to hide, right?"

"That's right. Also, if we move her, there's always the risk that he'll just wait us out. We can't hide her forever."

McNally thought for a moment. "All right. I'll approve this." Terri almost leapt from her chair, ready to take action as he held his hand up to slow her, pointing at both of them in the process. "But I want you two wired. Go downstairs and check out a couple of those Secret Service radio rigs, and maintain constant contact. I'd feel better if the Richmond field agents were taking care of this, but I think you'll just argue with me, so I'm giving you this. You're on a short leash here, Agent McKinnon. I never pegged you for the cowboy type, but you seem to believe that you have some insight here, so I'll have to trust that. Please don't give me any reason not to." With a wave of his hand, he indicated that they could go.

Terri practically shot from the office, but McNally stopped Bobby before he could follow her. While she waited for him, Terri slipped her computer into its bag, along with the case files, including the faxed pages from the Ann Arbor police. Her plan all along had been to drive to Mount Crawford to check on Jen. She'd gone as far as to suggest packing a suitcase just in case, which he had done. Terri was determined when she was on a mission. And she was probably right. They needed to be at Jen's house—to protect her and to bring this case safely to a close before anyone else was hurt. Terri was action girl, and she knew that Bobby trusted her enough to go along.

He finally came out of McNally's office. Terri couldn't stand it. "What was that all about?" she asked.

Bobby grabbed her by the elbow and dragged her toward the elevator, "That was about you, Agent McKinnon." He lowered his voice, "He told me to keep an eye on you."

She pulled out of his grip. "I'm fine, Bobby. Let's go."

"Just a second, Terri, we need to stop at the supply desk downstairs," Bobby said as he packed up his laptop. "I want to take a truck instead of my car."

"Good. There's more room in there anyway for our equipment."

They got to the basement and headed directly to the supply area. Checking out two earpiece/transmitter wires, they both shrugged out of their jackets and clipped the battery packs to their belts. Bobby helped Terri run the wires up her back, anchoring the one for the earpiece to her collar and running the other down her left arm for the microphone that attached to her wristwatch. After carefully pulling her jacket back on, she helped Bobby through the same procedure. As they signed for the radios, extra batteries, and the Chevy Suburban, the supply officer asked if they needed anything else.

Terri jumped on the request. "We need a Mossberg, two boxes of shells, and two Kevlar vests." She knew that Bobby was momentarily surprised at her request for the large shotgun, but his nod indicated he agreed that she was probably right, especially about the Kevlar, as she accepted the weapon and slipped the ammunition into her coat pockets. Unpredictable criminals were the worst kind, and the extra firepower and body armor would be welcome. Bobby grabbed the keys and the two vests and followed Terri back through the supply area and into the underground parking area where the vehicles were garaged. They made a brief stop at Bobby's car for their overnight bags, then found their loaner.

Terri stood by the truck, loading seven shells into the Mossberg 500 when the receiver in her left ear crackled to life. Bobby was testing the radio connection, and she heard his voice as if it was being piped directly into her skull.

"Mary One to Butch One, over." Her serious resolve was finally broken and she laughed, looking through the vehicle to where he was standing, talking to his watch, grinning like an idiot and pointing at her. "See, I knew you were still in there somewhere."

It proved to be the relief that she needed. She quipped back, testing her own voice-activated microphone, "Mary One, why do I have to be Butch One, over?"

He answered with a huge laugh of his own as she realized what he was pointing at and looked down at herself. She was standing, feet spread wide, talking to the left sleeve of her jacket with the butt end of a rather large shotgun sitting on her right hip. "Okay, I get it. Very funny. Let's get the hell out of here."

CHAPTER TWENTY-THREE

Bradley was several hours into his drive when he pulled into his third rest area, just north of Cincinnati, Ohio. His driving had been the picture of control, sticking to the speed limit as he constantly scanned the side of the road for the hitchhiker that would fit his requirements. He finally found his mark, sitting on a bench just outside the building that housed the rest rooms. A college student dressed in blue jeans, a bright red Cincinnati Bearcats T-shirt, and an Army field jacket. He smiled as he noticed the sign on the kid's backpack, simple cardboard with Sharpie lettering that stated his destination: Ft. Lauderdale, FL. Bradley couldn't help but remember his own college spring break trips to south Florida, begging money and rides along the way to get there. Too bad this kid wouldn't get exactly the trip he had planned.

He approached the kid, sizing him up for proper height and overall appearance. The kid watched as he walked up and pointed to the sign. "Need a ride?" Bradley asked.

The kid positively beamed. He would be perfect. "Yeah, that'd be great. You going all the way? To Florida, that is. I'm not offering anything but gas money."

Bradley smiled his warmest smile and said, "I'm going to Florida, but I have to make a side trip to Bowling Green,

Kentucky. If you can help me with a little something there, I can let you keep your gas money, and maybe even promise you some extra for your trouble. Sound good?"

The kid thought for a moment before agreeing. "Sure. Thanks, um…"

"Alan, just call me Alan." He extended his hand to the kid, who grasped it firmly and shook it. He released the kid's hand and started walking toward the car, gesturing for the kid to follow him. "Grab your stuff. Time to go." Just like shooting fish in a barrel.

❖

Terri and Bobby pulled into the gravel driveway in Mount Crawford a little before noon. The green 4Runner was parked next to the house. Terri had called to let Jen know that they were on the way so there would be no risk of surprise. She jumped out of the truck and asked Bobby to secure the vehicle and to come on in when he was ready. She wasn't even all the way to the side door when she was practically tackled by a joyous and very obviously relieved Jen. "Oh God, Terri. I'm so glad you're here."

Terri just held her, letting her cry off some of the tension. She finally let go enough to make eye contact, reaching up to hold Jen's face with her hands. "Are you okay?"

Jen actually let go of a laugh. "Compared to what? This isn't exactly my finest hour, you know."

Terri smiled and dropped her hands, relieved to see that the quirky sense of humor was still intact. "No, I guess it isn't." She stood back, barely getting out of the way before Bobby picked Jen up off the ground and squeezed her hard. He set her down and asked if she was okay.

"Again I say, compared to what? I guess I should feel

lucky. It's not every girl who gets to be the target of a homicidal maniac and then very nearly crushed by a huge gay man."

Terri instantly recognized the false bravado they'd had so many conversations about.

Jen chuckled. "Hey, I made you guys some coffee. So, you want to come in?"

They answered, a mix of "sure" and "thanks." Jen busied herself around the kitchen getting coffee mugs from the cabinet. Terri was still watching her with a strange mix of apprehension and arousal, wondering if Jen had actually gone to class in jeans, a button-down shirt, and skater-boy shoes. Since it wasn't her usual classroom drag, curiosity forced Terri to ask, "Jen, did you go to school today?"

"Yeah, I did. As soon as you called, I dragged myself off the floor over there and threw on something to wear. I was too scared to take a shower, so I opted to take myself out to breakfast at a really busy restaurant and then spent the entire morning around as many people as I could find."

Terri nodded, completely understanding Jen's fear of being alone in this situation.

"I mean I know he couldn't get here that fast, but I just couldn't stand the thought of being alone, even long enough to shower."

Terri closed the distance between them to give Jen another hug. "Well, we're here now." She angled her head to whisper as she let her hands slide down Jen's body, slipping them into the back pockets of the blue jeans. "I even brought a shotgun." She felt Jen's body lose some of its tension, melting into the words, and a whisper was returned.

"A big one?"

"Uh-huh…Mossberg 500 Tactical, seven round capacity, long barrel, pump action…" Terri punctuated the last two words with a slight forward motion of her hips.

"Oh, no, you two," Bobby said as he walked into the kitchen, waggling his finger with his best "get you, Mary" invocation. "This is not a booty call. We have work to do." Terri backed away, removing her hands from Jen's pockets, and raised her hands to indicate to him that she was clear. "Maybe later, after we get everything secure and get the county mounties in place." He pointed toward Terri specifically and said, "Don't forget about your leash, Agent McKinnon."

As Bobby left to retrieve the paperwork from the car, Jen mouthed the word "leash" and was promised an explanation later. Terri had more pressing issues to explain, specifically regarding her theories on the crime and why she believed that Jen was not the target, at least not tonight. Bobby returned quickly with the files. Jen was obviously distressed to see her own bad driver's license photo grinning from underneath the bold strokes of the numbers.

Jen suggested that since the FBI was now firmly ensconced in her home, maybe she could go take a shower while they called the county sheriff and explained the situation.

Terri watched her leave as Bobby, in turn, watched Terri. She knew that he was concerned, but was determined to leave it up to him to ask. She was not in the mood to act like a guest on *Dr. Phil* and just dump all her feelings on the kitchen table and be told that she was acting like an idiot. Fortunately, Bobby was far more understanding of her than she was of herself.

He finally broke the uncomfortable silence as Terri looked up the Rockingham County sheriff in the phone book. "Terri, sweetie, I know this is the most overutilized question of the day, but are you okay? I'm worried about you."

"I'm fine." He gave her his best I'm-not-sure-I-believe-you look, so she elaborated. "I am. Really. We're here, she's okay...well, not as okay as she claims, but she's unharmed. I think we know where Davis is, and I feel pretty much in control of the situation. If you'd just take a walk around the perimeter when the sheriff gets here, and give me a chance to really talk to her privately, I'd feel better yet."

He was still concerned. "It's just, this morning, I've never seen you act like that, but I get it. The fact that the rest of the office, especially McNally, noticed something is, well, unusual at best."

"Bobby, I'm going to let you in on a little secret. Every time we walk into a situation like this one, I'm scared to death. The only difference here is that I'm more concerned about her than I am about myself, so there isn't any energy left for me to build the walls to hide behind. I'm not really reacting any differently, I just can't cover it up. Does that make any sense?"

"Yeah, I do get it. I guess if I was trying to protect someone who looks at me the way she looks at you, I'd get a little crazy too. Just please be careful, okay?"

"I promise." She heard the shower start in the upstairs bathroom. "Can you please coordinate this stuff with the sheriff? Jen and I really do need to discuss some things about the house and the situation."

He nodded and pulled out his cell phone while Terri got up and paced around the kitchen. She stopped at the fridge to get a bottle of water when she noticed motion in the mudroom. Snickers had just come in through the dog door, so she went over to say hello and scratch him on the head. He launched himself at her, dancing on his back legs, begging for more attention. It was funny that he was so silent, given what she knew about the little mutt. She hoped it would be different if someone unwelcome arrived. A small canine alarm would be a nice addition to their arsenal.

Bobby finished his phone call and went to the mudroom to share the information with Terri. "They'll be here in five minutes. Someone was right down the road, so I'm going outside to wait for them." He checked his watch, noting that the time was getting close to one o'clock. "I figure we'll need at least half an hour, maybe a little more. There's a lot of open property here, but the sheriff has a map. Does that give you enough time?"

She looked at her own watch. "That should be fine. Is your wire turned on?"

He spoke into the cuff of his jacket. "Check, over. You good?"

She mirrored his action. "Check...we're good." She lowered her hand to speak normally. "Take your time. I want to know every way possible for him to get near this house."

He smiled at her as he placed one hand on the storm door. "You know I will. I'll be back soon." He added, with a wink, "Don't do anything I wouldn't do."

Terri didn't even have a chance to answer before he was out the door, leaving her to wonder if there was actually anything that he wouldn't do. She doubted it.

CHAPTER TWENTY-FOUR

Snickers went nuts when the sheriff arrived, growling and barking like Terri had never seen before. "I guess that answers that," she said to no one in particular. She closed the inside door, locked it, and watched as the officer got out of his car. He had that typical local cop swagger that she was so familiar with. She idly thought that maybe Snickers just didn't like straight people. That would explain his odd behavior. "Good thing Davis is straight, huh, Snickers?" She looked to the little dog. He was quiet again, looking at her with great interest as he propellered his tail in agreement.

"Terri, who are you talking to?" Terri had been so occupied that she didn't hear the shower turn off or Jen come back downstairs and head to the kitchen. "I just saw Bobby leave with the cops."

Terri was a little embarrassed. "Actually, sweetie, I was talking to your dog." She went back into the kitchen and found Jen standing next to the table, wearing a bathrobe, toweling off her wet hair. "He's a pretty good listener."

Jen finished with her hair and hung the towel over the back of the chair. "What was Bobby talking about when he said that thing about you and a leash?" She moved, scooting the chair aside to sit on the end of the table. "That was weird."

"Actually, Jen, I was a little, um, shall we say, insistent with everyone in the office this morning." Terri paused, looking for the right words to explain her out-of-the-ordinary behavior. "McNally suggested that I might be holding something back and questioned my objectivity, so he told me that I was on a short leash and told Bobby to keep an eye on me." She took a breath, searching for understanding in Jen's face. "I guess I really was kind of a bitch."

Jen took her hands, pulling her closer. "You were worried...about me, right?" She kept pulling until Terri was between her knees and her legs made contact with the edge of the table. "That's flattering."

Terri pulled her hands free to lightly stroke Jen's bare thighs, fighting a little to stay in the moment. "God, Jen, I actually called someone 'newbie' and sent him for coffee. No wonder everyone thought I was losing it." She shook her head and took a long breath, relaxing somewhat, and allowed herself to see the humor in the situation. "I felt awful afterward. I thought that poor kid was going to wet his pants, I scared him so bad." She started to laugh, but stopped as she felt warm hands slide under her jacket, pulling her even closer. "Jen, what are you doing?"

The hands didn't stop as Jen answered. "Listening to your story."

The hands traveled up her sides, avoiding her breasts until she felt fingers playing with the skin at the open collar of her shirt. Terri let go with a nervous laugh. "I don't think so."

She felt the fingers undo the first button below the open collar as Jen urged her to continue her story. "I'm hanging on every word."

Terri felt her shirt open a little wider as a soft, wet mouth took over for the fingers on the hollow of her throat. "Jen, you know I can't"—she gasped as the kiss became little bites, and the missing hands found a home on her ass—"can't concentrate when you do that."

The little bites stopped. "Agent McKinnon, you think too much." The little bites resumed.

Terri's head was swimming as she fought the sensations that were coursing through her body while the hands on her ass massaged and pulled her even tighter against the end of the sturdy table. She was losing the fight as her hands slid under Jen's bathrobe to caress the naked body underneath. "Jen, what are we…we can't…I'm supposed to be working." She gasped again as the hands on her ass slid around to lightly touch her breasts.

Jen scooted forward on the table, opening her legs just a little wider. "I think what we are doing would be considered completely inappropriate, panic-induced sex, and yes, we can." Terri's hands slid farther up under the robe, pulling it open to touch bare breasts. Jen gasped and tried to finish her thought. "Can't we just forget about"—she stopped the thought as her words were silenced with an insistent kiss, but resumed it again when breathing became necessary—"work?" Terri's hands were moving again, toward the thighs they'd left just moments ago. "Besides, work means keeping an eye on me, right?"

Terri could only nod, biting her lower lip as the light touches on her breasts became slightly more insistent pinches on her nipples through the fabric of her shirt and bra. Jen continued her observation. "So keeping an eye on me means that you should watch when I do this." She removed a hand from Terri's breast and used it to move Terri's hand from her thigh, guiding it toward the place where she needed it the most. "Are you watching?" Jen asked as Terri's hand found her incredibly wet pussy. Terri could still only nod and chew on her lip.

"Terri, do you see what you do to me?" Jen was panting out her words through gritted teeth. She pulled harder on the lapels, urging Terri to climb up on the table as she used her feet to slide back. "Can you see how bad I need you?" She lay back on the table as Terri got up on her knees, supporting her upper body with her left hand near Jen's head. Jen continued to pull at her lapels, looking her straight in the eye. "How bad I need you to fuck me?"

Terri obliged. She was oblivious to everything except the body moving beneath her wrapped tightly around her fingers. She was thrusting hard and fast as Jen continued to voice her needs. She felt a bead of sweat drip from her nose to land on the table. She heard Jen's breathless request: "More, please, I need more."

She added another finger, bringing the total to three, drawing out a long groan as she leaned close to Jen's ear. "Touch yourself for me."

Jen finally released the lapels she'd been clinging to for dear life, using her right hand to touch herself as requested. The combination of her own fingers on her clit and the three fingers pistoning in and out of her cunt was just too much to take. She threw her head back, banging it hard on the table, and loudly cried out the release of her orgasm. Terri didn't stop until Jen came a second time, even harder than the first, crying out again and pounding her free hand repeatedly on the surface of the table. She used that same hand to grab Terri by the arm, signaling that it was time to stop.

Terri hastily removed her fingers to check on Jen's condition. "Sweetie, are you okay? You really banged your head there."

Jen, still a little out of it, reached around to the back of her head, rubbing the spot and wincing. "God, I'm so smooth sometimes. What a spaz." She met Terri's concerned look.

"No, baby, I-I mean yes. I'm fine. Actually lots better than I was half an hour ago." She smiled a little noting that she truly was a little less worried. "Are you okay? Sorry, I was kind of pushy."

"Jen, it's fine. It's nice to have—" She stopped mid-sentence and her eyes grew wide in an expression of extreme shock. The shock was soon replaced by another expression that Jen couldn't quite identify as Terri lowered her head and hissed out, "shit." Jen continued looking for an explanation, but what she got instead was a brief, but very sincere apology. It only got more bizarre as Terri sat, turned around, and scooted to the edge of the table. Putting both feet on the floor, she raised her left hand toward her face, took a deep breath, and spoke into the sleeve of her jacket. "Field One, this is Base One, go ahead. Over."

It certainly didn't take a PhD from MIT for Jen to figure out what had just happened. She'd just been fucked stupid on her kitchen table by a government agent, coming so hard that she'd bashed a knot on her own head, and was evidently broadcasting it to the world via two-way radio. She could do nothing but laugh at the absurdity as she sat up and gathered the bathrobe around her. She scooted over to hug Terri from behind, but backed off a little as her still-sensitive crotch rubbed up against the holstered weapon in the small of Terri's back.

"Field One, give us five minutes, then head on in. Over and out." Terri held Jen's hands close to her belly as she spoke. "Well, this is certainly surreal." She turned her head to look at Jen, whose chin was now on Terri's shoulder. "Are you sure you're not mad? I just forgot. I told you not to distract me."

Jen kissed her on the cheek. "Nah, it's all good. It's my fault anyway. And it was certainly worth any amount of teasing and embarrassment I might have to suffer just to have you touch me like that." She ignored the gun pressing against her crotch to hug Terri tighter. "Anything's worth it if I get to be with you."

Terri laughed as she provided a small warning. "Jen, you might have to make good on that 'anything's worth it' part when Bobby gets back here. You know how he is."

"Ah, I can take him. Leave it to me." She leaned in to kiss Terri one more time. "I'd better go get dressed." Terri moved forward enough to give her room to jump off the table. She watched Jen grab her towel and leave the room, idly wishing there was time for a cold shower.

CHAPTER TWENTY-FIVE

Bradley drove the whole trip to Kentucky. He'd managed to keep the kid pretty quiet, between the fifth of bourbon he'd purchased in Cincinnati and the continuous supply of marijuana. The kid was so quiet, in fact, it was possible that he was unconscious. That suited Bradley just fine. He was not a big one for idle chitchat; he just wanted to get to Bowling Green by nightfall. There would be some time to kill, but he could just sit and wait while the kid slept.

He had everything in place. The three incendiary envelopes were in the trunk, the map of the location of the house was on the front seat of the car, and the tool kit to break into the basement window was in his jacket pocket. Oh, and the kid in the backseat. That was the best part.

Just outside of Bowling Green, and a little after midnight, he found the right road for the Mullins house. There were several other houses on the road, but they were far enough apart that he would be difficult to spot once he left the car. He pulled the car behind some bushes to hide it from view of the road and killed the engine. Reaching over the back of the seat, he poked the kid to wake him up. He was not unconscious, but he was really out of it.

"Kid, wake up. We're here." He shook him a little more to get him awake. "How you doing back there?"

The kid stirred, still more than a little inebriated. "I hear you…I'm up." His words were slightly slurred as he tried to speak. "God, I think my head's going to explode."

Bradley appeared to care, just for the sake of his passenger. "Sorry, kid. You hit that bourbon pretty hard. I'll get you a couple of pills for your head once we get to the house, okay?"

The kid rubbed his face with both hands and shook his head. He winced as if in pain as he answered, "Thanks, dude. I'm really hurtin' back here."

Bradley got out of the car and went around back to open the trunk. He found the three envelopes, still carefully folded in their Ziploc bag, and slipped them into the large pocket of his field jacket. He also took out a shirt similar to the one he was currently wearing, and closed the trunk. Moving around to the passenger side of the car, he opened the back door and tossed the shirt to the kid. "You need to change into that. I don't want you here looking like you've been hitching rides for three days." The kid peeled off his T-shirt and changed into the blue button-down, too drunk, stoned, and sick to care enough to argue.

Bradley asked the kid to repeat the plan one more time, making sure that he wasn't too loaded to understand. "Dude, it's like this. I'm going to help you sneak into the basement of your ex-wife's house so you can get some money that you hid there. She's going to be pissed if she knows you're there and call the cops because of some kind of restraining order." He looked at Bradley with bloodshot eyes. "Then I get behind the dryer, pry out the loose brick, take out the cash box, and then we split it, right?"

"You're a fucking genius, kid. That was perfect." Bradley

smiled his most genuine fake smile and helped the kid from the car, grabbing the discarded T-shirt on the way out. He had to support him with an arm around his waist until the kid got his legs under him. "Don't forget, she's probably home and in bed, so we need to be as quiet as we can."

The kid giggled and raised a finger to his lips in the universal sign of shh. "We'll be like sneaky cats." He lowered his hand and pulled down on the front of his shirt in an attempt to tidy himself a little. "Gotcha. I'm ready."

Bradley didn't answer as he pulled the kid along toward the house. He saw a car pull down the road, but they were far enough away to avoid being seen. Once the taillights were out of sight, he quickened his pace, helping the kid across the road and into the bushes that marked the property line of the house. He held the kid's head down as he scanned the darkness and lights of the house for signs of activity. Everything was quiet. He used the cover of the bushes to traverse the distance of the property to the place where he needed to be. Fortunately, there was a small creek that provided a low spot to travel through, so they were both able to get to the bushes at the side of the house without being spotted. The kid tried to ask a question, but Bradley stopped him with a hand over his mouth. He raised his own finger to his mouth in a perfect imitation of the kid's earlier gesture, and the kid got the point, nodding his head in understanding. Bradley put his hand in his pocket and pulled out a pill bottle. He shook out four Percocet, offered them to the kid and urged him to swallow them with the remaining bourbon that he'd so thoughtfully remembered to bring along.

Bradley saw the perfect window at the rear side of the house. He pulled the kid along, stopping just before they got to the window. He dropped low on his belly and looked inside. He couldn't see much because it was dark inside, so he removed the tool kit from his pocket and used the flashlight to look around through the window. Still no movement. He took a glass cutter from the kit, applied it to the window with its suction cup, and cut a small circle in the window, close to the latch. Once that was accomplished, he turned to the kid and pointed with his free hand for him to open the window, then climb through and into the basement.

Bradley had to hang on tightly to the kid to get him though the window with as little noise as possible. He could tell that the bourbon and Percocet were starting to work their magic as the kid wobbled, dangerously close to falling over as his feet touched the basement floor. Bradley backed into the window behind him and guided him to a pile of laundry in the middle of the floor in front of the dryer, adding the kid's red Bearcats T-shirt before arranging the pile with his feet so the kid could lie down and pass out. He used the flashlight briefly to look over the rest of the basement, noting the locations of several large piles of boxes. It was all too perfect.

One last touch. He removed a Glock and silencer, identical to his own, and a wallet from the pocket of his jacket, swapping the kid's for a new one that contained his own authentic Michigan parole card and driver's license, and put it into the back pocket of his now-unconscious hitchhiker. The Glock fit perfectly down the back of the kid's pants. He slipped the kid's wallet into his own jacket, scanned outside for movement, and climbed out the window.

Sitting on the ground up close to the house, he removed the three envelopes from his pocket and worked quickly. He laid the envelopes out flat, grabbed all three by the clasp end, and shook the pool chemicals into the Brylcreem. The chemical reaction started immediately, and the envelopes grew hot in his hands. He leaned into the window far enough to Frisbee the packets, one by one, into the piles of boxes around the perimeter of the basement. Then he ran like hell toward the woods in the opposite direction from his car. He stopped behind a tree just long enough to catch his breath and watch the flames in the basement burst into life, spreading an eerie glow around the foundation of the house.

He only had to walk a half mile back into town, find the rental car place, and hit the road again. He'd head north to Elizabethtown and find a place to crash for a few hours. He had all of his belongings in his pockets, including his handgun and enough cash to purchase anything else he would need. And then it was on to Virginia to finish this thing once and for all.

CHAPTER TWENTY-SIX

Terri awoke with a start. She was disoriented and unable to remember falling asleep. Since the darkness outside offered little assistance regarding the time, she attempted to roll over to check the time on the clock next to the bed. Finding that she was pretty much pinned to the mattress, half under a sleeping Jen, she contented herself with turning only her head to see the clock. Five twenty-two a.m. Staying right where she was seemed the most appealing plan, but her bladder was going to make that impossible. She slid out from under Jen as gently as she could and offered her pillow up as a suitable replacement. Jen hugged tight to the pillow, mumbling, "Mmm, smell good," or something like that, and continued sleeping.

Terri walked softly around the end of the bed and went into the bathroom, closing the door behind her before turning on the light. Wincing as the bulbs came on over the medicine chest, she raised one hand to shade her eyes until they became accustomed to the brightness. Catching her own reflection in the mirror, she looked hard at herself, making special note of the dark circles under her eyes. "God, Terri, you look like shit." She knew that exhaustion was taking its toll on her, but there'd be time to rest when this was all over.

Terri finished in the bathroom, turning out the light before she opened the door. Jen was still fast asleep, but she'd managed to kick her covers off and was curled up like she was cold, despite the sweatpants and T-shirt that she was wearing. It was warm in the house, in contrast to the cold outside, but Terri decided to pull the covers back over her anyway, tucking her in with a kiss to the top of her head. Terri really wanted to climb right back into the bed, but hearing that Bobby was up, she pulled Jen's purple hoodie on over her tank top, took her gun from the drawer of the night table, and slipped the P-228 into the large pocket on the front of the sweatshirt.

She went downstairs to the kitchen and found Bobby toasting a bagel and waiting for the coffee to finish brewing. He looked up from the toaster and registered her appearance with a bit of surprise and concern. "God, Terri, you look like shit."

She registered his comment with a grimace, but had to agree. "I know. I've had this same conversation with myself already, thank you." She rubbed her face with both hands, still trying to clear some of the cobwebs. "I just need some rest."

Bobby offered her the bagel he'd been preparing, but she declined it and took a seat at the side of the large table. "No, thanks. How long till coffee?"

"Just a couple more minutes." He was still watching her with concern. "Terri, you should go back to bed. The sheriff will be back in an hour. I can cover until then." Bobby had agreed to take the night watch, leaving Terri with the day shift, both backed up by the local sheriff.

"Nah, I don't think it'll help anyway. I feel like I could sleep for the next week and it still wouldn't be enough. I'll just dose with some coffee and try to keep moving." It sounded good in theory, but her body just wouldn't cooperate. She crossed her arms on the table and laid her head down, not sleeping, but not quite awake either.

"You might want to be careful there...don't want to fall asleep and bang your head on the table."

Try as she might, she didn't have the energy for a witty retort, so she satisfied herself with an evil, tight-lipped, don't-go-there glare. He just smiled as she let her head fall forward onto its resting place on her arms. She probably would have stayed that way for a very long time, but startled awake as the phone went off in her pocket. She sat up to remove the offending device, noticing that the caller ID indicated that it was the office. She flipped it open. "Agent McKinnon."

The voice on the other end was a familiar one. "Terri, it's Dave Stansfield. We've got some news." She sat up a little bit, shrugging off the sleepiness and urged him to continue. "There was a fire in Bowling Green, Kentucky, last night that you need to know about."

Terri was confused. "Okay. What does that have to do with anything?" Terri was trying not to be terse with Dave, but she was too tired to give it much effort.

"Apparently, the house was owned by an employee of NoVaGenEx, and the fire department found a body in the basement. It was pretty mangled in the blaze, but physical description and the contents of a wallet identified the victim as one Bradley Allen Davis of Ann Arbor, Michigan. It would seem that your perp managed to get loaded and torch himself in his own fire."

Terri was floored, to say the least. "Are they sure it's him?"

"Yep, the basic body type, you know, height/weight stuff was right. The fire got most of the rest of anything else we can use." Terri wrinkled her nose as she realized it meant that the coroner had nothing left to determine hair and eye color. "The wallet was damaged, but they found most of a Michigan driver's license and a parole card. It sure looks like him. Well, more like a pork roast now, but it used to look like him."

She swallowed hard as the image of a burnt and mangled corpse planted itself in her head. "Did they do any lab work?"

"Yes to that one too. High concentrations of alcohol, THC, and oxycodone. No wonder he passed out. Coroner thinks the combo would have killed him even without the fire. They won't finalize the report until the DNA stuff comes back, but you know the drill. Two to three weeks for results." She was well aware that DNA testing was still slow, but the other things would be enough for the coroner to make a preliminary report on identification and cause of death.

"Thanks for the info. Has McNally seen it yet?" Terri was hoping to avoid that conversation for at least a couple more hours.

"No. He's in meetings this morning, so he probably won't get it until ten or eleven. Unless you want me to call him."

"No, please don't call him. We've still got some things to finish up with here and Bobby's been up all night. I'd like him to get some sleep before we drive back." Terri was getting antsy and ready to end the call. "Call me if you have anything else. Oh, and fax the report to the number that I left on my desk, would you? Thanks, Dave."

"Hey, no problem."

She muttered an additional thank-you to Stansfield and snapped her phone closed. Bobby was incredibly patient during the call, but jumped as soon as she was done. "Davis is dead?"

Terri nodded and answered his question. "It would seem that way." She filled him in on the details that Stansfield had given her.

"You're not sure?"

"I should be. The evidence is all there, but I can't help but wonder…" She paused for another moment, searching for the right way to voice her concerns. "Bobby, it's just this: Davis has been meticulous about everything he's done. No clues, no hints, no stray fibers, nothing to tie anything to him except the numbers, and those only meant something to him and Jen. He managed to keep us in the dark for weeks, remember? And now, on the eve of his grand finale, he pulls a Marilyn Monroe and gets so hammered that he roasts himself in his own fire. Doesn't that sound the least bit off to you?"

"It does seem off. A little too convenient. Are you thinking decoy?"

"Yes, that's exactly what I'm thinking."

Terri stared out the window at the barn, shrouded in fog that reflected eerily in the moonlight, and tried to fill in the blanks. Movement on her left caught her attention, and she looked up to see a sleepy Jen standing in the doorway. Jen yawned and scratched her head, adding more crazy features to her already-interesting bed hair. She came into the kitchen, rubbed Bobby lightly on the back, and leaned over to give Terri a kiss.

Bobby said good morning and asked, "How's your head?"

Jen didn't bat an eye. "Great, how's your ear?"

He shot it right back at her. "Couldn't be better."

Terri just stared at them before she covered half of her face with one hand. "Oh, God, you two. Please don't start this already." They both smiled their warmest smiles at her as she stared back with her one uncovered eye. Jen was the one who broke the moment with a question.

"Why is it still dark outside and why are we talking about Marilyn Monroe?" She left the question in the air as she went to get coffee. Bobby told her the news about the fire and the body, but left Terri to fill in the details since she'd been the one on the phone. Jen seemed a little puzzled. "And we're not happy about this why?"

"Terri thinks it's bogus. You know, criminal-mastermind-fakes-own-death-for-dramatic-climax kind of bogus."

"That's really twisted and sick. But it is kind of clichéd. So does that mean the FBI officially thinks this thing is over? And what exactly does that mean? Will they make you two go back to the office?" Jen was getting more and more agitated with each question. "Oh, oh, maybe they could just tie me to a stake in the front yard and slap a big ol' red bull's-eye sticker on my forehead. You know, like that poor goat in *Jurassic Park*. Except he didn't have a sticker. Well, maybe he did, and we just didn't get to see it. Oh, and I guess there's no tyrannosaurus either, but hey, we have a chain-smoking homicidal whackjob arsonist to fill in for that part." She finally ran out of breath. Bobby just stared at her in amazement.

Terri immediately shifted into nobody-messes-with-my-girl mode, turning to take Jen's chin with one hand, forcing her to make eye contact. "Jen, look at me. No one is going to tie you out in the front yard, either with or without a sticker. I'm not going anywhere, and I really don't give a shit what McNally has to say about it. Bobby should probably go, but I'm here until I get a DNA report from Kentucky that tells me I'm wrong and Davis is really dead." She turned to Bobby, silently asking what he would do.

He became the picture of resolve, looking directly at Jen as he answered and pointed at Terri. "She stays, I stay. Simple as that. You two are going to need me since we lose the sheriff patrols when McNally calls. I can take the hit. It's way better than the alternative." He switched his attention to Terri. "Also, I'm supposed to be keeping an eye on you. McNally said so."

Jen mouthed a silent "thank you" while Terri took his hand and expressed her gratitude out loud. He waved them off with an "aw, shucks" look. "Besides, there's free porn on the radio here. I'm not going anywhere."

CHAPTER TWENTY-SEVEN

Bradley took his time driving through Kentucky. He stopped, as planned, for a nap, but he was so juiced from his success with the fire that he made it all the way to Lexington. There was still seven hours' worth of expressway between him and his goal, plus an hour or two for stops, but he'd bought himself some time with the body switch in Bowling Green. He also knew that DNA testing took a couple of weeks and that the FBI would certainly figure out what really happened, but he'd have his problem solved by then. The feds would call their people back, and everyone would be happy that he was gone. Except he wasn't really gone. This was still too easy.

Bobby and Terri were working at the kitchen table when the dreaded phone call from McNally came. It was close to ten thirty. Jen had earlier excused herself to get some work done in her office, but Terri knew it was more of an attempt to give her and Bobby some space to work their "g-man mojo." Jen always had a way of putting things that brought a smile to Terri's face, but she wasn't sure she had the mojo to pull this off. Not this time.

When the call came in, Bobby offered to do the honors, but Terri declined, reasoning that she wanted to face McNally sooner rather than later, and that she'd feel better once it was done. She paced the floor as she explained her theory about the body switch. Every now and then she caught Bobby's eye and could see even his normal patience was reaching an end. She tried to telegraph her reaction to let him know what was happening on the other end of the call. With one final "Yes, sir, I understand," Terri snapped her phone closed and set it on the table.

"He said we get forty-eight hours. He also said there's not enough here to justify local backup, so we need to cut them loose. If nothing has happened by noon Friday, we're supposed to head back to the office. I guess that's something."

"Terri, it's more than something. At least he was willing to listen to you."

"Well, it wasn't easy. And believe me, that leash that he has around my neck just got a lot shorter." It suddenly struck her that Bobby was up, and hadn't gotten any sleep, except for a short nap, since before he took the watch the previous night. "You should get some sleep before tonight, don't you think?"

He opened his mouth, no doubt to protest, but closed it again. "I suppose you're right. I'm kind of doing the walking dead thing here. Just a few hours, though, okay?"

Terri was surprised he was willing to do that much, but he had to be exhausted. She certainly was, and she'd managed to squeeze in a few hours of rest the night before. "Okay, I'll get you up, say, around four o'clock. It'll still be light outside, and I'll try to have some kind of an action plan pieced together by then."

Bobby scratched his head and yawned. "Are you sure about this? I can sit up long enough to work some details out. It's really no big deal."

"No, Bobby. I know by now what you would do in this situation, and I don't think Davis is a broad daylight kind of guy. No, please get some rest. I need you alert later."

Bobby poured his cup of coffee back into the pot and started for the stairs. He stopped in the doorway and turned to face her. "If you two decide that you need to work off some tension, please keep it down. I've had enough details to hold me for a while." He didn't give her a chance to answer as he trudged through the living room and up the stairs to the guest room. Terri knew right then and there how exhausted he really was if that was the best shot he had to throw at her.

She only had a minute to think on that before Jen returned to the kitchen, crossing to the counter to refill her coffee. "Did you finally get him to go to bed?"

"Yes, he finally gave in." Jen leaned back on the counter and studied Terri's face. Terri met her gaze and said, "I know what you're thinking, and I'm fine. I actually got some sleep last night. I'll be fine."

Jen brought her cup of coffee to the table and sat. She raised a hand to Terri's face, stroking her cheek lightly with her thumb. "You know, I'm the false bravado gal here. You don't have to do that for me."

Terri took the hand from her face and kissed Jen's palm. "I know, but I do have to do it for me. There's a lot here to think about and McNally only gave us forty-eight hours to work with. Not that I'm leaving if nothing happens, but I really don't think we're going to need more time than that."

"Why do you think that?"

"I just think that Davis's little decoy stunt in Kentucky means he's ready to make his final move." Jen shuddered, fully aware of what his final move was meant to be. "He must know that DNA testing takes time but that we'll eventually find out that the body wasn't his. I also think everything he's done since he made his phone call from Ann Arbor means that he's starting to burn his bridges and he'll just keep moving forward with his plan."

Jen hugged herself, rubbing at the goose bumps that had surfaced on her arms. Terri waited patiently as Jen tried to verbalize her concerns, placing her hands on Jen's, helping to ease the chill that she knew instinctively was fear rather than cold. The words weren't coming, so Terri tried to help her along. "Jen, what's going on with you?"

Jen hesitated, lowering her eyes and shifting her feet. "Do you think it makes me a bad person because all I can think about is, well…" Terri urged her forward with a look. "All I can think about is how much I want you to blow this guy away? Does that make me, I don't know, like him, somehow? Like I want someone to hurt him for doing all of this."

"Oh God, Jen, no. You caught him doing something illegal ten years ago. He was guilty as hell, and he deserved what he got. You aren't to blame for any of this, but I know you still feel responsible for it. I'd actually be surprised if you felt any differently at all." She paused to let the words sink in and allowed herself a small smile. "Besides, I've already blown him away at least five different ways in my own head. Do you think that makes me a horrible person?"

Jen's tension visibly eased and she managed a little laugh. "No, I think that makes you my knight in shining armor. Unfortunately, that makes me your damsel in distress, and I really don't like the way that feels. It's kind of itchy." She wiggled a little to prove her point.

"Well, I can help with the itchy part…later. Right now, we've got work to do." Terri picked up a pen and turned her attention to the legal pad. "Tell me everything we need to know about your house."

❖

Bradley was tired, but glad to finally get where he was going. He'd been on the road since early in the day, and he was ready to take a break and savor this one last evening before he took care of everything, once and for all. He continued northward on I-81, passing the Mount Crawford exit, smiling at the sight. Just a few more hours.

He continued on to Harrisonburg, where he figured he'd treat himself to a nice dinner. Crossing through the light on Market Street, he pulled into the drive for the Red Lobster. He could have a nice plate of scampi and a glass of wine while he gave his road-weary brain a rest.

Terri now knew the location of the box for the electrical system, the shutoff for the propane tank, and every way on or off the property. While the land was mostly open, the house was easily defended. Three outside doors and the large bay window were the most vulnerable, but also easily guarded. That would make it difficult for someone unwanted to get in. She decided that it was best for Bobby to take the perimeter watch outside, just because he stood a better chance of detaining Davis if he ran into him first, most likely by turning him into a human tent stake and pounding him into the ground. Terri would take the immediate perimeter of the house, moving farther out if Bobby needed her. They would both be wearing their wires, so she took extra time making sure that Jen knew this fact and could behave accordingly. They would also both be outfitted with their Kevlar body armor. Better safe than sorry. Terri was inwardly kicking herself a little that she hadn't checked out a third vest for Jen, but if Davis got close enough to her, the vest would most likely become a moot point. She also decided that the Mossberg needed to come into the house with her. After a final check of the ammo, she stashed the shotgun and the extra rounds in one of the large cupboards in the mudroom.

Terri was just getting ready to go upstairs to wake Bobby when he appeared in the kitchen doorway, looking a little more rested than he had earlier. "I set the alarm on my phone. I was afraid you'd feel sorry for me and let me keep sleeping." He stretched one last time and headed for the coffeepot.

"Sorry, Bobby. Not today. I was actually just getting up to wake you. Do you want to see the plans?"

"Anything complicated or tricky? Or just basic patrol and wait?"

"Pretty much patrol and wait."

"The best way into the yard from the unfenced property is up through the barn. I think I need to concentrate my efforts down there, and you just stay close up here."

Terri readily agreed, but added an additional warning. "Jen says that the restoration work isn't done in the barn yet, so be careful if you need to go in there, because there are still some weak spots in the floor." Bobby agreed that they were covered as best as could be expected. The sheriff was still available but not making routine patrols, so they both programmed the Rockingham County emergency number into the speed dial of their phones, just in case backup was needed.

They were so wrapped up with their planning that they failed to notice that Jen had evidently finished her work in the office and returned to the kitchen. "Hey, you guys, what should I do?" She crossed her arms over her chest and rolled her eyes. "Well, besides scream like a little girl and hide, that is." Bobby and Terri looked back and forth between Jen and each other, not sure of the answer.

Terri continued to think as Bobby finally came up with an idea. "Have you ever fired a weapon?"

Jen could only laugh at Bobby's question. "The last time

I tried to shoot a rubber band at somebody I managed to hit myself in the eye. So the answer to that question is a really big no."

Terri giggled at the image, but sensing Jen's discomfort at the firearm idea, stifled it with a hand over her mouth. "Sorry, sweetie."

"It's okay. Remember, spaz here. One of my greatest strengths is that I know what my weaknesses are." She moved nearer to the table to stand behind Terri, using her hands to work some of the kinks out of Terri's neck and shoulders. Terri visibly relaxed into the touch, making little mewing noises as some of the tension was worked away.

Bobby just watched, pointed at Terri, and spoke to Jen. "Looks like you know some of her weaknesses too."

She winked at Bobby. "Buddy, you have no idea."

He winked back. "Care to enlighten me?"

Terri had to put a stop to this line of conversation before it went someplace she really wasn't prepared for it to go. "C'mon, you two. Play nice. We really do need to stay focused here." She patted the hands that were still on her shoulders. "How about if you two reheat some of those leftovers from last night while I go upstairs to take a shower and try to wake up."

Chapter Twenty-eight

Terri turned off the water and pulled back the curtain. The shower had gone a long way toward recharging her batteries, which had been running dangerously low. She dried off her hair and wrapped herself in a fluffy white towel, making eye contact with her reflection in the partially steam-covered mirror. The dark circles under her eyes had diminished but were still present. She brushed her hair out just enough to keep it from becoming a tangled mess, and pulled it back into a wet ponytail. Satisfied that she was ready to go, she turned off the bathroom lights and went into the bedroom. She jumped, startled by the presence of another person in the room. It was Jen.

"Sorry, I didn't mean to scare you." Jen was sitting on the edge of the bed, but made no move to come any closer. "You seem kind of jumpy."

"I'm okay…well, maybe just a little jumpy." She pulled the towel tighter around herself. "Did you need something?"

"I just wanted to see you alone…you know, before the thing tonight." Terri smiled, thankful for the company. "Can I stay while you get dressed?"

Terri walked over, leaving wet footprints in her wake, and sat next to Jen on the bed. "You can stay as long as you like."

She turned enough to get both arms around her and held her, desperately needing the simple touch that the hug provided. "Jen, you know that we're going to get through this, right?"

Jen laughed, but just a little. Apparently she wasn't convinced. "Anything you say, Agent McKinnon." She patted Terri on the knee. "You'd better get dressed. You're far too naked and I'm way too nervous to be trusted with that. Go on."

Terri got up from the bed and went into the dressing area where she'd put her luggage earlier. She pawed through the stuff she'd packed, opting for white cotton undergarments and the comfort they provided. She dropped the towel and changed into the bra and panties, fully aware of the eyes that followed her every move.

"Jen, you still back there? It's awfully quiet." Terri heard the soft *mm-hmm* as she pulled a black turtleneck on over her head. She stepped into her black cargo pants and then grabbed a pair of short, white cotton athletic socks, slipped them on followed by her black leather sneakers, lacing them up tight with double knots. Next came the heavy leather belt, with holster attached. She threaded the leather through the belt loops of her cargos, checked the magazine of the P-228 one last time, slid it back into the gun, and slid the weapon into its holster at the small of her back. A flashlight and handcuffs followed, tucked safely away in the cargo pocket of the pants. Each article of clothing, each piece of equipment settled her nerves that much more, made her feel more like the professional she knew she was rather than the scared girlfriend.

The two-way radio was next, but she required assistance. Terri clipped the battery pack to her belt and walked back over to the bed. She held the wires out to Jen and told her what to do while she secured her watch to her wrist. Jen ran the first wire up her back, clipped the coiled cord of the earpiece to the collar of the turtleneck, and held the second wire while Terri attached the microphone to her watch. Terri then went back to the dressing area to retrieve the Kevlar vest, pulled it on over her head, cinched up the Velcro straps, and readjusted the radio wires. The last thing in her luggage was her FBI issue black nylon jacket. She slipped it on and turned to face Jen, who was, as expected, ogling Terri decked in her battle gear.

Terri smiled, leaving the smart remarks for a better time, and came closer, taking Jen by the hands, pulling her up and off the bed, and holding her close. "Jen, I promise you, this will all be over soon, and we'll all be happy and alive, and still talking about it when we're old and gray."

She felt Jen pull her closer and nestle in under her chin. "You can't know that for sure." Terri felt Jen trembling in her embrace.

Terri pulled back and took Jen by the upper arms. "Jen, please…Would someone who can put on all this shit," she looked down at herself for emphasis, "and still look this hot, possibly say anything to you that wasn't true?"

Jen smiled her first genuine smile of the evening. "No, I guess not." Jen's eyes freely roamed up and down Terri's body. "You do look incredibly hot, by the way."

Terri sighed. "It's the cross I bear."

She leaned in for a warm, wet kiss, took Jen by the shoulders, turned and propelled her toward the door. She stopped to grab the extra clips for her weapon, and Jen hesitated in the doorway, pointing at her. "Old and gray, you promise?"

"Yes, I promise. Now go on. Let's go eat before Bobby gets all of it."

❖

Bradley left the restaurant where he'd stopped for dinner and drove the fifteen minutes to the house in Mount Crawford. Just to be safe, he decided to make one pass of the building and property. He turned off the main road, tires bumping hard as he hit the dirt and gravel of Scholars Road. After another mile of washboard dirt and tractor ruts, he found the house, identified by a standard white mailbox with the correct house number. He didn't slow down below the twenty miles per hour that the lousy surface allowed, but he wanted to because he couldn't believe what he saw sitting in the driveway. A large black Chevy Suburban with U.S. government license plates.

The feds weren't supposed to be here.

Terri had been standing outside for what seemed like hours. Probably because it actually had been several hours. It was cold. Not the windy, bitter cold that she had become used to growing up in the farmlands of southwestern Ohio, but cold nonetheless. She stamped her feet and rubbed her hands together to warm them up, wondering to herself why she hadn't taken the time to dry her hair. She spoke softly into the air at no one. "I'll probably get the damn flu or something. That's all I need." It was time to take another walk around the house. She left her spot on the dark corner of the front porch, hanging in the shadows as she passed the side entrance, and quietly swung the gate open to head into the large, fenced-in area that served as the backyard.

She stayed close to the house and approached the screened-in back porch. A small scraping noise alerted her from within the house, so she slid her hand under the nylon jacket and wrapped her fingers around the butt of the handgun nestled in the small of her back. The noise became more pronounced and she realized that it was someone whispering, trying to get her attention. "Psst, Terri. Don't shoot. It's me."

Terri released her hold on the weapon and scooted over closer to the porch. "Jen?"

Jen was sitting on the floor, hiding in the shadows of the waist-high plywood that made up the lower portion of the walls of the screen porch. She whispered, "Yeah, it's me. I brought you some coffee." A steaming mug appeared through the flexible dog door and found its way onto the top step. "I thought you might be cold."

Terri was slightly annoyed, even though she was glad to have some company. "Jen, you're supposed to be upstairs."

"I know. I've been sitting up there in the dark for hours and I had to pee. I took a chance and came down here to see what was going on." She paused as Terri came over to the step to get the coffee. "What *is* going on?"

Jen crouched low in the shadows and took a drink, warming her hands on the sides of the mug. "Nothing. Bobby's been checking in every fifteen minutes, but we've still got five hours' worth of nothing."

As if on cue, Terri's earpiece crackled to life. "Base One, this is Field One. Terri, I heard something in the barn. Probably just a cat, but I'm going to check it out. Over."

She answered, whispering into the sleeve of her jacket. "Field One, understood. Over." Terri turned her attention back to the disembodied voice on the back porch, and whispered, "Bobby heard something in the barn. He's heading down there now. You should go back upstairs."

She handed her coffee mug back through the dog door, felt as her hand was squeezed from the other side, and heard one last small whisper, "Terri, please be careful." The hand released her, and she knew that Jen was crawling back into the house through the shadows, closing and locking the interior door of the house behind her.

Terri continued her perimeter patrol, turning the corner that led to the bay window side of the house. Every light was turned off, making the house appear to be empty, but she was still able to detect movement within as Jen sneaked low, avoiding the windows, through the living room and back up the steps.

❖

Bradley was forced to revise his primary plan. That was really too bad because it was so simple. Just ring the doorbell, say hello, maybe have some coffee and catch up a little, and then blast a neat little hole in the back of her skull. The FBI was supposed to be gone. They should have found the kid's body in the basement. He had done everything right, but the FBI was still here. Something was definitely wrong, and he was pretty sure that it had something to do with Agent McKinnon.

Well, it couldn't be helped. He thought hard, fighting the rising pain in his head. He couldn't afford to medicate now; he had to stay sharp to outwit these government types.

He parked his rental car over the rise of the hill, about three-quarters of a mile east of the property. The barn was the first thing he would come to, as well as being the easiest access through the fenced-in part of the yard. He walked, scooting from tree to tree, holding his dark jacket closed with his left hand, clutching an automatic weapon in his right. Approaching the barn, he entered on the lower level and immediately ran into a stack of old gardening tools, knocking them over in the process. He winced at the clatter, stopping completely to listen for other sounds. He turned on his flashlight and scanned the area quickly for any other obstacles. Seeing none, he slipped his handgun into the back of his pants, dimmed the flashlight, picked up a rusty shovel, climbed the steps that led up to the main level of the barn, and selected a bale of straw to hide behind as he tried to spot the location of the FBI agents on the property.

Heavy footsteps sounded on the floorboards, heading directly toward his hiding place. He waited patiently as a large man approached, stopped, and turned to head back toward the front door of the barn. Bradley let him get about halfway back to the exit before he made his move. He moved silently from behind the bale of straw, took three or four carefully placed steps, pulled the shovel back, and did his best imitation of Babe Ruth knocking a high fastball out of the park.

As the agent pitched face first, unconscious, to the floorboards, Bradley set down the shovel and apologized. "Sorry, big guy, nothing personal. This isn't about you." Scooting back behind his bale of straw, Bradley quietly waited for the person he knew would be coming next.

❖

Terri startled when she heard the commotion in the barn. It sounded to her like something metallic striking something solid, followed by the sound of a large object hitting the floor. She tried to reach Bobby on the radio, but there was no response. Weapon drawn from the back of her jacket, she moved as quickly and quietly as possible, without running, to the source of the noise.

The main entrance to the barn was like a bridge spanning a small dip in the ground that led to the downstairs entrance of the large building. She opted for the lower entrance since the wide ramp to the large open door provided her with absolutely no cover. After half sliding down the hill to the lower door, she pushed it open as gently as possible, cringing as it squeaked on its rusty hinges. It was pitch black in the musty bowels of the barn, so Terri dug out her flashlight and twisted it to bring the bulb to life. Stepping over the threshold, she swung the beam of light around the area, making sure that her weapon was pointed the same direction, and stopped as she found the steps that led up to the main level of the rickety old building. There was still no motion anywhere in the barn, and she was getting concerned that she'd left the house unguarded, so she tried Bobby on the radio again.

"Field One, this is Base One, over." Nothing. "Field One, come in please, over." Still nothing. "Shit. Bobby…Come in." The silence was deafening as she felt the panic start to rise. Fighting it down, she headed carefully up the steps. She swung the light around the area, coming to rest on a large dark mass lying among the scattered straw on the floor. The shape was all too familiar, and the impact of that sight slammed into her painfully. It was Bobby, and he wasn't moving.

Her own adrenaline kept her moving forward as she crossed the space to check on Bobby. Crouching low on the ground, she checked his neck for a pulse. Relief followed when she felt the strong beat beneath her fingers and finally noticed the steady rise and fall that indicated he was still breathing. Quickly scanning the area, she spotted the shovel lying on the ground next to Bobby's unconscious form, and immediately became aware that the shit had finally hit the fan, and she was left alone to deal with it.

Before she even had a chance to pull her phone out of her pocket to call the sheriff for assistance, she sensed a presence behind her, and before she could turn to see what that presence was, she felt the one thing that every agent feared the most. The business end of an automatic handgun pressed to the soft flesh at the back of her neck. She gasped and froze as a cocky voice that she'd heard once before on the telephone spoke to her with a cheery nonchalance that made her blood run cold.

"Agent McKinnon."

Terri swallowed hard as the hammer of the gun was cocked back, feeling it click as it locked into place.

"It's so nice to finally meet you in person."

CHAPTER TWENTY-NINE

Terri didn't move. She could barely breathe. The muzzle of the weapon pressed against her neck never wavered as Davis stood there. Her legs were beginning to cramp as a result of the awkward position she was in, half kneeling, half squatting. Her finger itched at the trigger of her own weapon, still in her right hand, as she contemplated her next move. Now, if she could only figure out what the fuck that next move was.

Davis finally started to talk. "Agent McKinnon, I must say I'm surprised to see you here. More specifically, you and your rather large friend. I would have thought that my little decoy stunt in Kentucky would have had a bit more impact. It seems I have underestimated you, and that's a problem."

Terri gritted her teeth, fighting hard against her panic and rage. Figuring that he was looking for a question from her, she obliged. "Why?"

"Why?" Davis was incredulous, quickly becoming agitated. "Because I had one thing to do, and you've made it harder than it needed to be. This could have all been so simple if you could have left things alone and let them play out the way they were supposed to."

Losing the fight against rage, she growled out her next question. "And let you kill her?"

Davis was starting to come unglued. "Yes, let me take away her life just like she took away mine." He pressed forward with the handgun for emphasis, spitting out his next question. "Don't you get that?"

Terri was grasping in her head for the right answer that would keep Davis from blowing her brains out when she spotted something moving peripherally in her vision, approaching the barn from the direction of the house. Since she couldn't see, she could only hope that Davis had his back turned and was completely unaware that there was an extremely agitated little dog streaking down the hill, ready to remove the stranger's foot from his ankle. Terri waited for the precise second when Snickers began to bark to make her move.

Davis's attention wavered for just a second, long enough to process that something was behind him, and Terri sprang into action. Jumping up from her crouch, she swung her right arm back in a wide arc, hand still clutching her weapon. She caught him hard in the side of the face with her wrist, missing his jaw with the butt end of the gun, shocking him far more than the appearance of the canine cavalry did. He tensed as the blow landed, and pulled the trigger of his gun. The blast hit Terri low on her rib cage. The Kevlar vest stopped the bullet, but the impact broke several ribs and knocked her from her feet with its force. It twisted her in the air, dropping her hard on the floorboards, face first, opening a large cut over her right eye. She struggled to take a breath against the red-hot bolts of pain that shot through her injured right side.

Davis had recovered somewhat, turned fully away from her, and was now squeezing off shot after shot toward the sound that had distracted him. Snickers was apparently smart enough to know that bang trumped woof every time, and he darted off to hide in the underbrush near the barn. Before Davis had a chance to realize what was happening, Terri was crawling fast, feet sliding on the loose straw, struggling to turn her body in an attempt to return his fire. She heard a loud crack, recognized immediately that it was not gunfire, but didn't have time to react as the weakened floorboards of the old building gave way, dropping her hard onto the packed earth of the lower level of the barn. As she cried out against the pain and struggled not to lose consciousness, she became dimly aware of laughter followed by the sound of footsteps quickly leaving the barn.

Gritting her teeth against the pain-induced nausea and vertigo, Terri hauled herself to her feet and lurched toward the open door of the lower level of the barn. She was still clutching her handgun, hugging her gun arm close to support her injured ribs. She emerged at the bottom of the small hill that she'd slid down just moments before, and scrabbled up it, pulling herself into the main part of the back yard. Using the back of her left hand to wipe away some of the blood that was running into her eye, she spotted Davis in the moonlight as he ran toward the house, knowing there was no way she could catch up before he got there. She could only pray that he did something stupid once he arrived, or this whole thing could be over soon in a really bad way.

Terri kept an eye on him as she struggled up the hill to the house. The gash made it hard to see, the broken ribs made it difficult to breathe and impossible to run, but she kept going, making the best speed possible.

❖

Bradley pulled the back door open and stepped up onto the screen porch. Using his elbow to break the glass, he reached in, unlocked the interior door, and went into the house. His head was pounding, threatening to explode. It was dark inside and he was unfamiliar with the layout of the house. He only went a couple of paces before he tripped over a rug in the mudroom, swearing through clenched teeth as he struggled to keep his footing. "Fuck this," he said, turning on the light from the first switch he found. Overhead fluorescents blinked on, illuminating his path toward the one thing that he needed to locate. He hesitated for a moment, allowing his eyes to become accustomed to the light and the hot spikes of pain to level out in his head, and turned to head into the kitchen.

There was only one doorway that led into the rest of the house, so he followed the trail, stopping in the living room long enough to turn on one small lamp. Still no one. He rattled the locked door to the office, but stopped when he heard a voice upstairs, just loud enough to bring a smile to his face. "Terri, baby, is that you?"

He didn't answer. Smiling, he flipped on the light and started up the stairs, slowly, stepping as lightly as possible toward the sound of that voice that he remembered so vividly. The voice of the person he'd spent the last ten years dreaming about, and there was nothing that could keep him from her now.

❖

Terri couldn't risk following him into the house, so she moved as quickly as her injuries would allow past the back door, through the gate, and around to the front of the house. She fought the nightmare images playing through her head. Images of losing everything to a stranger with a gun. Terri couldn't do this again.

But she had to. She forced down her fear and willed herself

to act like the professional that she knew she was. Experience told her that her best shot would come from the front yard as he headed up the steps. There were large windows in both bedrooms, as well as an even larger window at the top landing of the stairs, and Davis had so thoughtfully provided enough light for her to watch every move he made.

She had the advantage that the spotty cover of darkness provided between the patches of light spilling out of the windows, so she made her way painfully over to the trunk of a large maple tree, leaning against its rough surface for support as she made one last half-successful attempt to wipe the free-flowing blood away from her eye. Barely able to lift her arm from her shattered right side, she supported her gun hand with her other hand and took as deep a breath as she could muster in an attempt to calm the painful shaking and line up for the shot.

❖

Bradley arrived on the landing at the top of the stairs, swiveling his head to determine which bedroom the voice had emanated from. He turned to his right just in time to come face-to-face with someone in the doorway. With more than a little amusement, he watched as the face that had haunted his every waking and sleeping moment appeared with a trace of a hopeful smile, and morphed quickly to an expression of wide-eyed terror. Before Jen could register what was happening, he grabbed her by the front of her shirt, forced her back against the door frame, and pulled up his gun, slowly turning it just enough to allow him to place the muzzle snugly up against the opening of her left nostril. "Well, well. Dr. Rosenberg. Look at you, all grown up." He pulled tighter on her shirt. "Remember me?"

Jen nodded, trying to move as little as possible, as Bradley continued to taunt her. "Terri, baby?" He actually laughed, but just a little. "I love that you're screwing the FBI. Good for you. I certainly can't blame you. That Agent McKinnon would definitely be a trip that I'd like to take." He tilted his head and leaned in closer to her face, pushing for a reaction. "Too bad I had to shoot her."

The reaction was not what he expected. He watched as her eyes left his and looked over toward the window that he realized too late was right behind him. He released his hold just enough to turn, lowered his weapon, and asked, "Who's out there?"

❖

Terri watched the intense interplay through the window. She fought hard against her own panic and almost blinding pain to keep her weapon trained on the psychotic killer who was holding Jen against the door frame of her own bedroom with a loaded gun up her nose. Moving just a little to adjust her sweaty grip on the automatic weapon, she squeezed her left eye closed to line up the sights on the slide of the gun. Everything played out in close-up slow motion as Davis released Jen and turned to see what was outside.

She barked out an order—"Jen, get down!"—and pulled the trigger. The blast and resultant recoil of the weapon drove her arm back, sending lightning bolts of pain through the right side of her body, driving her to her knees and forcing her to gasp for air. Visually, she followed the shot up to the window, straining again but finally losing the fight to remain conscious.

❖

It all went south so quickly. He heard the voice outside and saw Jen throw herself to the floor, covering her head with her arms. He turned back to try to catch her, but was stopped as the glass of the window shattered inward and something slammed hard into the center of his back. Fighting to breathe against the intense pain that ripped through his chest, he looked down to watch the red stain rapidly spreading out on the front of his light blue button-down shirt. He struggled to make sense of what had just happened. "My shirt…"

He crumpled to the floorboards as fragments of glass continued to rain down on him. Jen shakily pulled herself up by the door frame and shouted down at him, releasing all of her terror and fury in a single outburst, taunting him one last time.

"Who's out there? That was my girlfriend, you asshole."

CHAPTER THIRTY

Terri was still moving a little slower than normal. She puttered around the kitchen of her townhouse, making tea and scooping kibble. As Jojo happily began munching, Terri grabbed a white ceramic mug with bright rainbow letters that proclaimed her to be the "World's greatest girlfriend." She smiled at the sight of her new favorite mug, remembering the first time she saw it, overflowing with flowers, sitting on the tray table as she woke up in room 335 of Rockingham Memorial Hospital. That was ten days ago. The first two days were spent in the hospital where Jen had never left Terri's side, not even when the nurses suggested that she should.

Terri turned back toward the stove and reached up to select a variety of tea from the cabinet overhead. She winced as a fresh bolt of pain shot through her side, reminding her that things were still not quite right. She pulled her arm down, hugging it close against her injured ribs, remembering the doctors had told her that she'd probably still have some discomfort for at least a month. "Ow." She tugged at the hospital-issue rib support binding and started the process over again, this time using her left hand to reach up and remove the bright green Plantation Mint box.

She debated going back upstairs to check the news on

the Internet, but stopped when she noticed the time on the microwave. She smiled. It was almost three in the afternoon and she knew Jen would be arriving any minute. The pain was gone now, replaced by the flapping of butterflies in her belly. She couldn't wait to see Jen.

The FBI had graciously given Terri and Bobby time off to recover and finish their final reports on the Davis case from home. The reports were filed, their wounds were healing, and life had slowly returned to normal. Jen had had a week of classes to get through, but then she got ten days off for spring break, and was now on the way, Snickers in tow, to spend the entire time in DC.

The doorbell rang. Terri headed toward the front of the house and the commotion as Jen struggled, wrestling with her laptop case, large wheeled suitcase, and a really wiggly little mutt straining against his leash. Jen dropped the luggage, released the dog, and let the computer bag slide down her arm to the floor. Snickers immediately spied Jojo staring wide-eyed from the doorway to the dining room and bolted after her, grateful to have something to chase after being cooped up for two hours in the car. Jen and Terri just laughed and shook their heads, moving closer together to say a proper hello. Jen held her arms out, not sure what to do, so Terri took her by the hands, pulled her close, kissed her softly, and backed away. "Jen, you can touch, you just can't squeeze."

Jen still didn't seem convinced. "I don't want to hurt you. I saw what you looked like in the hospital. That was the nastiest bruise I've ever seen. Not to mention thirteen stitches and that incredibly sexy black eye."

Terri recalled her own images of what she'd looked like in the hospital. It really wasn't very pretty.

She took Jen by the hands and pulled so their bodies were touching. "Jen, sweetie, I'm really lots better now. I even got my stitches out yesterday." Just to demonstrate her much-improved physical condition, Terri pressed forward, offering a much longer and deeper kiss than the first one. As she felt Jen start to relax, she ended the kiss, smiled a little, and said, "See? Much better. Now, why don't you grab your stuff and we'll take it upstairs? I've got something I want to show you."

Terri led her up the steps to the second floor and into the bedroom. Terri sat on the edge of the bed, needing a moment to rest. Jen sat, placed a tentative arm around Terri's shoulders, and leaned in carefully to give her a quick kiss. She noticed the large business envelope sitting on the nightstand. "Is that what you wanted to show me?"

Terri smiled and grabbed the envelope, presenting it with great ceremony. Jen turned it over. "Go ahead, open it."

Jen undid the metal brads that held the envelope closed and pulled out the single sheet of paper. It was a certificate, homemade on the computer but fashioned to look official. She grinned as she read the proclamation out loud. "Federal Bureau of Investigation Certificate of Valor, presented on this date to Snickers Rosenberg, for bravery above and beyond the call of duty." Jen looked up from the certificate, sniffing as the tears began to flow. She laughed. "He'll love this. Thank you."

Terri was beginning to feel a little teary herself, so before the entire scene could get weepy, she pointed to a bag leaning against the side of her dresser. "I got him a frame too. I figure he deserves at least that much for saving my ass out there in your barn."

Jen shuddered, recalling Terri's tale of what had transpired that night. "Terri, baby, I can't even begin to think what could have happened if Snickers hadn't been such a loudmouth that night. Please, please promise me you'll never get shot again."

"Promise me you don't have any other old friends out there that want to kill you."

"Fair enough." Jen raised her right hand. "I swear to you that I have no other skeletons in my closet that wish me dead." She added a resolute nod for emphasis.

"Understood." Terri took Jen's hands and looked her directly in the eye. "I promise that I will do my best to make sure I never get shot again. It wasn't much fun, believe me." She was reminded of that fact as her rib support shifted, causing her to flinch. Before Jen could react, she said, "I'm okay. It just slips once in a while. Don't worry about it."

"Are you sure you're okay?" Jen pulled back to look Terri in the eye. "You need to take it easy. Come here. Lie down with me."

"I could do that." Terri happily complied while Jen patted the comforter. Once on her back, Terri pointed to her shoulder. "You, right here." Jen snuggled in as instructed and made a happy noise. Terri thought it was the most wonderful sound she'd ever heard. She closed her eyes, and for the first time in a very long time, she let go of the past and thought about the future. Only this time, Terri wasn't afraid. She had hope. She had Jen.

"So, Agent McKinnon, what happens next?"

Terri smiled. "Anything you want, Dr. Rosenberg."

"Cool."

About the Author

D.L. Line has been many things at different times in her life: a musician, a pharmacy technician, a bartender, a student, a restaurant owner, a marching band director, and a dog sitter to name a few. Through it all, she has always been a storyteller.

D.L. lives in Virginia with her family, including Snickers the Wonderdog. *On Dangerous Ground* is her first novel.

Books Available From Bold Strokes Books

Erosistible by Gill McKnight. When Win Martin arrives at a luxurious Greek hotel for a much-anticipated week of sun and sex with her new girlfriend, she is stunned to find her ex-girlfriend, Benny, is the proprietor. Aeros Ebook. (978-1-60282-134-7)

Looking Glass Lives by Felice Picano. Cousins Roger and Alistair become lifelong friends and discover their sexuality amidst the backdrop of twentieth-century gay culture. (978-1-60282-089-0)

Breaking the Ice by Kim Baldwin. Nothing is easy about life above the Arctic Circle—except, perhaps, falling in love. At least that's what pilot Bryson Faulkner hopes when she meets Karla Edwards. (978-1-60282-087-6)

It Should Be a Crime by Carsen Taite. Two women fulfill their mutual desire with a night of passion, neither expecting more until law professor Morgan Bradley and student Parker Casey meet again…in the classroom. (978-1-60282-086-9)

Rough Trade edited by Todd Gregory. Top male erotica writers pen their own hot, sexy versions of the term "rough trade," producing some of the hottest, nastiest, and most dangerous fiction ever published. (978-1-60282-092-0)

The High Priest and the Idol by Jane Fletcher. Jemeryl and Tevi's relationship is put to the test when the Guardian sends Jemeryl on a mission that puts her not only in harm's way, but back into the sights of a previous lover. (978-1-60282-085-2)

Point of Ignition by Erin Dutton. Amid a blaze that threatens to consume them both, firefighter Kate Chambers and property owner Alexi Clark redefine love and trust. (978-1-60282-084-5)

Secrets in the Stone by Radclyffe. Reclusive sculptor Rooke Tyler suddenly finds herself the object of two very different women's affections, and choosing between them will change her life forever. (978-1-60282-083-8)

Dark Garden by Jennifer Fulton. Vienna Blake and Mason Cavender are sworn enemies—who can't resist each other. Something has to give. (978-1-60282-036-4)

Late in the Season by Felice Picano. Set on Fire Island, this is the story of an unlikely pair of friends—a gay composer in his late thirties and an eighteen-year-old schoolgirl. (978-1-60282-082-1)

Punishment with Kisses by Diane Anderson-Minshall. Will Megan find the answers she seeks about her sister Ashley's murder or will her growing relationship with one of Ash's exes blind her to the real truth? (978-1-60282-081-4)

September Canvas by Gun Brooke. When Deanna Moore meets TV personality Faythe she is reluctantly attracted to her, but will Faythe side with the people spreading rumors about Deanna? (978-1-60282-080-7)

No Leavin' Love by Larkin Rose. Beautiful, successful Mercedes Miller thinks she can resume her affair with ranch foreman Sydney Campbell, but the rules have changed. (978-1-60282-079-1)

Between the Lines by Bobbi Marolt. When romance writer Gail Prescott meets actress Tannen Albright, she develops feelings that she usually only experiences through her characters. (978-1-60282-078-4)

Blue Skies by Ali Vali. Commander Berkley Levine leads an elite group of pilots on missions ordered by her ex-lover Captain Aidan Sullivan and everything is on the line—including love. (978-1-60282-077-7)

The Lure by Felice Picano. When Noel Cummings is recruited by the police to go undercover to find a killer, his life will never be the same. (978-1-60282-076-0)

Death of a Dying Man by J.M. Redmann. Mickey Knight, Private Eye and partner of Dr. Cordelia James, doesn't need a drop-dead gorgeous assistant—not until nature steps in. (978-1-60282-075-3)

Justice for All by Radclyffe. Dell Mitchell goes undercover to expose a human traffic ring and ends up in the middle of an even deadlier conspiracy. (978-1-60282-074-6)

Sanctuary by I. Beacham. Cate Canton faces one major obstacle to her goal of crushing her business rival, Dita Newton—her uncontrollable attraction to Dita. (978-1-60282-055-5)

The Sublime and Spirited Voyage of Original Sin by Colette Moody. Pirate Gayle Malvern finds the presence of an abducted seamstress, Celia Pierce, a welcome distraction until the captive comes to mean more to her than is wise. (978-1-60282-054-8)

Suspect Passions by VK Powell. Can two women, a city attorney and a beat cop, put aside their differences long enough to see that they're perfect for each other? (978-1-60282-053-1)

Just Business by Julie Cannon. Two women who come together—each for her own selfish needs—discover that love can never be as simple as a business transaction. (978-1-60282-052-4)

Sistine Heresy by Justine Saracen. Adrianna Borgia, survivor of the Borgia court, presents Michelangelo with the greatest temptations of his life while struggling with soul-threatening desires for the painter Raphaela. (978-1-60282-051-7)

Radical Encounters by Radclyffe. An out-of-bounds, outside-the-lines collection of provocative, superheated erotica by award-winning romance and erotica author Radclyffe. (978-1-60282-050-0)

Thief of Always by Kim Baldwin & Xenia Alexiou. Stealing a diamond to save the world should be easy for Elite Operative Mishael Taylor, but she didn't figure on love getting in the way. (978-1-60282-049-4)

X by JD Glass. When X-hacker Charlie Riven is framed for a crime she didn't commit, she accepts help from an unlikely source—sexy Treasury Agent Elaine Harper. (978-1-60282-048-7)

The Middle of Somewhere by Clifford Henderson. Eadie T. Pratt sets out on a road trip in search of a new life and ends up in the middle of somewhere she never expected. (978-1-60282-047-0)

Paybacks by Gabrielle Goldsby. Cameron Howard wants to avoid her old nemesis Mackenzie Brandt but their high school reunion brings up more than just memories. (978-1-60282-046-3)

Uncross My Heart by Andrews & Austin. When a radio talk show diva sets out to interview a female priest, the two women end up at odds and neither heaven nor earth is safe from their feelings. (978-1-60282-045-6)

Fireside by Cate Culpepper. Mac, a therapist, and Abby, a nurse, fall in love against the backdrop of friendship, healing, and defending one's own within the Fireside shelter. (978-1-60282-044-9)

A Pirate's Heart by Catherine Friend. When rare book librarian Emma Boyd searches for a long-lost treasure map, she learns the hard way that pirates still exist in today's world—some modern pirates steal maps, others steal hearts. (978-1-60282-040-1)

Trails Merge by Rachel Spangler. Parker Riley escapes the high-powered world of politics to Campbell Carson's ski resort—and their mutual attraction produces anything but smooth running. (978-1-60282-039-5)

Dreams of Bali by C.J. Harte. Madison Barnes worships work, power, and success, and she's never allowed anyone to interfere—that is, until she runs into Karlie Henderson Stockard. Aeros EBook (978-1-60282-070-8)

The Limits of Justice by John Morgan Wilson. Benjamin Justice and reporter Alexandra Templeton search for a killer in a mysterious compound in the remote California desert. (978-1-60282-060-9)

Designed for Love by Erin Dutton. Jillian Sealy and Wil Johnson don't much like each other, but they do have to work together—and what they desire most is not what either of them had planned. (978-1-60282-038-8)

Calling the Dead by Ali Vali. Six months after Hurricane Katrina, NOLA Detective Sept Savoie is a cop who thinks making a relationship work is harder than catching a serial killer—but her current case may prove her wrong. (978-1-60282-037-1)

Shots Fired by MJ Williamz. Kyla and Echo seem to have the perfect relationship and the perfect life until someone shoots at Kyla—and Echo is the most likely suspect. (978-1-60282-035-7)

truelesbianlove.com by Carsen Taite. Mackenzie Lewis and Dr. Jordan Wagner have very different ideas about love, but they discover that truelesbianlove is closer than a click away. Aeros EBook (978-1-60282-069-2)

Justice at Risk by John Morgan Wilson. Benjamin Justice's blind date leads to a rare opportunity for legitimate work, but a reckless risk changes his life forever. (978-1-60282-059-3)

Run to Me by Lisa Girolami. Burned by the four-letter word called love, the only thing Beth Standish wants to do is run for—or maybe from—her life. (978-1-60282-034-0)

Split the Aces by Jove Belle. In the neon glare of Sin City, two women ride a wave of passion that threatens to consume them in a world of fast money and fast times. (978-1-60282-033-3)

Uncharted Passage by Julie Cannon. Two women on a vacation that turns deadly face down one of nature's most ruthless killers—and find themselves falling in love. (978-1-60282-032-6)

Night Call by Radclyffe. All medevac helicopter pilot Jett McNally wants to do is fly and forget about the horror and heartbreak she left behind in the Middle East, but anesthesiologist Tristan Holmes has other plans. (978-1-60282-031-9)

Lake Effect Snow by C.P. Rowlands. News correspondent Annie T. Booker and FBI Agent Sarah Moore struggle to stay one step ahead of disaster as Annie's life becomes the war zone she once reported on. Aeros EBook (978-1-60282-068-5)

I Dare You by Larkin Rose. Stripper by night, corporate raider by day, Kelsey's only looking for sex and power, until she meets a woman who stirs her heart and her body. (978-1-60282-030-2)

Truth Behind the Mask by Lesley Davis. Erith Baylor is drawn to Sentinel Pagan Osborne's quiet strength, but the secrets between them strain duty and family ties. (978-1-60282-029-6)

Cooper's Deale by KI Thompson. Two would-be lovers and a decidedly inopportune murder spell trouble for Addy Cooper, no matter which way the cards fall. (978-1-60282-028-9)

Romantic Interludes 1: Discovery ed. by Radclyffe and Stacia Seaman. An anthology of sensual, erotic contemporary love stories from the best-selling Bold Strokes authors. (978-1-60282-027-2)

A Guarded Heart by Jennifer Fulton. The last place FBI Special Agent Pat Roussel expects to find herself is assigned to an illicit private security gig baby-sitting a celebrity. (Ebook) (978-1-60282-067-8)

Saving Grace by Jennifer Fulton. Champion swimmer Dawn Beaumont, injured in a car crash she caused, flees to Moon Island, where scientist Grace Ramsay welcomes her. (Ebook) (978-1-60282-066-1)

The Sacred Shore by Jennifer Fulton. Successful tech industry survivor Merris Randall does not believe in love at first sight until she meets Olivia Pearce. (Ebook) (978-1-60282-065-4)

Passion Bay by Jennifer Fulton. Two women from different ends of the earth meet in paradise. Author's expanded edition. (Ebook) (978-1-60282-064-7)

Never Wake by Gabrielle Goldsby. After a brutal attack, Emma Webster becomes a self-sentenced prisoner inside her condo—until the world outside her window goes silent. (Ebook) (978-1-60282-063-0)

The Caretaker's Daughter by Gabrielle Goldsby. Against the backdrop of a nineteenth-century English country estate, two women struggle to find love. (Ebook) (978-1-60282-062-3)

Simple Justice by John Morgan Wilson. When a pretty-boy cokehead is murdered, former LA reporter Benjamin Justice and his reluctant new partner, Alexandra Templeton, must unveil the real killer. (978-1-60282-057-9)

Remember Tomorrow by Gabrielle Goldsby. Cees Bannigan and Arieanna Simon find that a successful relationship rests in remembering the mistakes of the past. (978-1-60282-026-5)

Homecoming by Nell Stark. Sarah Storm loses everything that matters—family, future dreams, and love—will her new "straight" roommate cause Sarah to take a chance at happiness? (978-1-60282-024-1)